Praise for *Restoring Christmas*

"*Restoring Christmas* is a tug at your heart, laugh out loud, wonderful read for Christmas!"

Debbie Macomber, #1 *New York Times* best-selling author

"I absolutely loved *Restoring Christmas* and love Cynthia's captivating writing style. The book was filled with all the things you want in a Christmas story: charming characters, beautiful reminders of the best holiday traditions, and a plot that keeps the tension building all the way to the end, which is—like Christmas stories of old—filled with wonderful and satisfying surprises. Keep the tissues handy. Highly recommended."

Dan Walsh, best-selling author of *The Unfinished Gift* and *Remembering Christmas*

"Reading *Restoring Christmas* is like settling in with a plate of frosted cookies and a cup of hot tea on a snowy afternoon—perfectly satisfying. While it's a short novel, the characters are nicely developed and the story well-paced. There are enough twists and turns to keep the reader guessing and an ending that's likely to cause a few happy tears. *Restoring Christmas* is sweet without being sappy, charming without being cliché, and faith-filled without being preachy. Get your Christmas fix today!"

Sarah Loudin Thomas, author of the Inspy Award-winning *Miracle in a Dry Season*

"This charming Christmas story should come with a warning label: BEWARE: You will not want to stop reading once you begin. Cynthia Ruchti has done it again, introducing the reader to a delightful cast of characters and spinning an endearing story of restoration and love. I give it 2 thumbs up!"

Kendra Smiley, conference speaker, author, and radio host of *Live Life Intentionally*

"Come in from the cold, wrap up in this tale, and sit back as your heart fills with hope right along with Alexis, Gabe, Elsie, and the Fieldstone House. A master builder of stories, Cynthia Ruchti has taken the splintered edges of life, gathered them close with grace, and using her trademark tools of symbolism and character, constructed a refuge of healing to find shelter in this season. *Restoring Christmas* glows warmth into the darkness of winter with soul-deep themes, heart-stealing sparks between characters, a thread of mystery to intrigue and inspire, and just as the title promises, the restoring joy of Christmas."

Amanda Dykes, author of the critically-acclaimed
Bespoke: A Tiny Christmas Tale

"Sometimes restoring an old stone house is merely the means to reveal and restore hurting souls. Let the engaging *Restoring Christmas* open your heart to the beauty of both Christ's coming and your own restoration. A wonderful read!"

Gayle Roper, author of *Sea Change* and *Special Delivery*

"Thank you, Cynthia Ruchti, for creating another delightful fiction experience. As a fan of old houses and makeover stories, I was enthralled with this story of a home renovation that restores hope and the spirit of Christmas along with an old stone house you'll want to call home. A touch of humor, a thread of romance, and the backdrop of a snow-blanketed Wisconsin town makes *Restoring Christmas* the perfect December read . . . or all year 'round."

Becky Melby, author of the Lost Sanctuary series

"Ruchti's well-chosen words drew me into the story until I believed I was there, entangled in the graceful subtleties, the humor and heartache. The love."

Davalynn Spencer, author of *The Wrangler's Woman*

"Yes, the Christmas holidays can be difficult. How many of us are walking around in need of a restored Christmas? Hope restored? Our past converted into something more suitable for how we live today? You simply must read the unfolding of this satisfying and sweet romance from exquisite storyteller, Cynthia Ruchti. I can't believe I cried at the end . . . but restoration is like that sometimes."

Lucinda Secrest McDowell, author of *Dwelling Places*;
encouragingwords.net

"Cynthia Ruchti's *Restoring Christmas* restores my hope in a season challenged by false expectations. I laughed aloud, spurted some tears, and rejoiced throughout the memorable book. Fabulous characters, witty writing, and a winsome plot combine to create the perfect Christmas read. Good for your heart and your hope levels."

Jane Rubietta, international speaker and author of
Finding Messiah and *Worry Less So You Can Live More*

"*Restoring Christmas* made me laugh out loud as well as cry in the same paragraph! Cynthia's mastery of dialogue allowed me to fall in love with Alexis and Gabe and cheer for the healing necessary in Elsie's heart. By the end of the book, Hope House was not just a place in a book but a destination I wanted to go to. I am already planning on buying Christmas gifts for all of my book loving friends."

Becky Turner, National Managing Partner for The Barnabas Group
and global business and spiritual "fixer upper" specialist

"Cynthia Ruchti writes directly to the heart of women. Her characters face life in ways that instantly endear and engage readers. *Restoring Christmas* shows how challenges and restoration go hand-in-hand in such a way that you won't want to put this book down. Cynthia Ruchti truly delights!"

Cristel Phelps, bookseller

"The key to award-winning author Cynthia Ruchti's special talent is to transform the ideal depiction of Christmas into a truly restorative story that evokes the real meaning of Christmas with charm and eloquence. She takes the meaning of 'restoring Christmas' to God's higher, deeper meaning. I highly recommend *Restoring Christmas* to read each Christmas season!"

Dianne Burnett, former fiction editor for Christian Book Distributors

"I was not prepared for the depth that Ruchti plumbs into each character, scene, and description. Every word is hand-picked to build the themes of control and letting go, listening or doing, covering or celebrating flaws, and the impossibilities that only God can overcome. Cynthia hits her stride in *Restoring Christmas*, her best yet. Readers will be wanting to hire Alexis and Gabe for their next restoration project, which I hope Cynthia already has planned!"

Wanda Erickson, Regional Library Director

"Cynthia Ruchti writes fiction that touches people's hearts. Her work is often as significant as what professional counselors do in their therapy sessions to heal people's emotional wounds. I highly recommend her novels."

Dr. Judith Rolfs, author and licensed family counselor

Restoring Christmas

CYNTHIA RUCHTI

WORTHY®
Inspired

Published by Worthy Inspired, an imprint of Worthy Publishing Group, a division of Worthy
Media, Inc., One Franklin Park, 6100 Tower Circle, Suite 210, Franklin, TN 37067.

WORTHY is a registered trademark of Worthy Media, Inc.

HELPING PEOPLE EXPERIENCE THE HEART OF GOD

eBook available wherever digital books are sold.

Library of Congress Control Number: 2016950176

ISBN 978-1-61795-707-9

Cover Design: Melissa Reagan
Cover Image: Doug Menuez | Getty Images

Printed in the United States of America

1 2 3 4 5 6 LBM 20 19 18 17 16

DEDICATED TO THE PEOPLE IN MY LIFE

WHO REVIVE THE BEAUTY

ETCHED IN OLD THINGS

And from the window
Candleglow
Reflected in
New-fallen snow
Recalling a Christmas
Long ago
So very long ago

CHAPTER ONE

ROASTED CHESTNUT LATTE? How can that be a bad thing?

Alexis Blake shuffled forward in line as two of the three customers ahead of her finished paying for their beverages. The only person left now in the chasm between her and coffee stepped up to place his order. A defensive linebacker–sized guy with espresso-colored hair curling over his collar. Alexis caught sight of the chalkboard boasting the Caffé Tlazo breakfast special of the day. Wild mushroom and crispy shallot quiche. Not her typical organic yogurt and blueberry quick-fix breakfast. And not what she expected from an unpretentious café in an unpretentious town along the western shore of Lake Michigan.

Algoma. She rehearsed it in her head for the sake of any sensitive locals: *Al (as in Pal) GO-muh.* The town might have shared Lake Michigan with Chicago more than two hundred miles to the south, but it had little else in common with the metropolis. Alexis hadn't seen much more of shore-hugging Algoma than what edged the road that brought her to town. The highway wove through farmland and orchards, slowing her down with interspersed villages clustered around a cheese factory, winery, or connection to the "Old Country."

She'd sat at the stop sign in Algoma too long where Highway 54 decided it was done, the highway creators as startled by the view as she was, apparently. The road teed with a wide-sweeping vista of Lake Michigan and the curious, skinny, red lighthouse at the tip of the breakwater. Turning south at the tee would have taken her toward Kewaunee by way of Alaska. The town, not the state. North led to the heart of her destination, home to the most important client she'd never met. Would soon meet. Right after Alexis signed the contract with the videographer.

After a flood of email exchanges, she was about to meet the local videographer who could either propel her career forward or ruin it.

While she waited for the linebacker to finish gabbing with the barista, she checked the clock on her phone. Fifteen minutes. She had fifteen minutes to place her order and get settled before George Langley arrived. Not much breathing space, but the drive from Green Bay, across the stubby base of Wisconsin's thumb, took longer than expected. As had picking out an outfit that said "confident but approachable." She unbuttoned her wool coat. Late October. Too warm for wool. Too cold for a lighter jacket.

Alexis scanned the customers already seated. As eclectic a mix as the artsy décor. Nobody matched the description of the George Langley she'd seen on the website, a man with silver hair, distinctive bushy eyebrows, and sparkling deep-water eyes.

The chatty guy in front of her turned after slipping a dollar into the tip jar and headed toward the small, mismatched tables scattered throughout the compact café. A room that looked as if it had lived an earlier life as a screened-in porch held additional tables and chairs—slate-topped wrought iron, patio-style.

No. No, no, no. The ex-football player chose the one table he couldn't have, the one by the windows in the southeast corner. The spot where she and George were destined to plot out the next eight weeks of her life, and maybe longer. Maybe the next eight, ten, twenty years, if the audition video went well. No. This guy could *not* have that table.

She corrected the details of her fumbled order—her fault—focused on the task at hand, added more to the tip jar, and launched herself toward the corner table.

"Excuse me, sir. Would you mind moving to another spot? I'm meeting someone here." She tapped the slate tabletop with her index finger. "Here."

"No can do."

Nice smile. Nice try. "I'd really appreciate it. I've never met the man before and . . . "

"Blind date, huh? *Breakfast* blind date?" He nodded as if contemplating. "Uncommon, but not unwise."

A waitress set a blue-green and chocolate brown pottery mug in front of the irritant. The foamed milk on top sported a design that looked like a cross between a heart and a fern leaf. *Classy touch.*

"It's a business meeting," Alexis said, pulling her laptop case off her shoulder as if that would convince him.

"Me, too. Here. Right"—he tapped with his index finger—"here."

"Couldn't you just—" She surveyed the room. "There's an empty table in the other corner."

"Yes. I'm sure you'll be completely comfortable there for your 'business meeting.'"

Was it so hard to believe she was a professional? Well, on her way to becoming a professional? She removed her coat and slipped it over the back of the chair she wanted. The chair she intended to occupy. That ought to convince him. Her "confident yet approachable" black suit jacket and sweater paired with her favorite copper statement necklace ought to let him know she was there for serious discussion, not romance.

The linebacker leaned forward. "You connected with him on the Internet, didn't you?"

"Technically, yes. But not in the way you're thinking. He's—"

The man shrugged. "Sometimes it works out."

Was he trying to cheerlead for her dating life? Or volunteer to be her life coach?

"And sometimes," he said, leaning back, "you wind up with a man totally different from what you expected." He sipped his coffee drink and dabbed at the resulting foam mustache with the cloth napkin. It was still wrapped around his eating utensils.

Alexis sighed and glanced at the entrance. No one matching the face, age, or graying hair of the videographer had arrived yet. She still had time to—

"Why don't you wait here?" He pulled out the chair draped with her coat. "I don't have to move. You can still connect with what's-his-name. Win-win."

She stood her ground, weighing the idea.

The barista approached with her roasted chestnut latte. "Where do you want me to put this?"

"Miss Blake is joining me here." Moustache Man tapped the table. "Right here."

That smile. That "is he serious?" smile—wait. He knew her name? Oh. The tag on her laptop case. "Fine. Yes. I'm sitting."

She took a third chair rather than the one offered and wrapped her hands around her mug, seafoam green with a drizzle of coppery glaze near the lip. Handcrafted mugs. Interesting. If the coffee was as good as it smelled, she might find this a frequent stop during her term in Algoma. But first—

"You're not George Langley." Definitely not. But those eyes. She'd seen them before.

"He's my dad."

"That's who I'm meeting. I'm Alexis Blake. I'm hiring him to do a project for me." The dot-to-dot connecting lines swerved between points. "I don't have to tell you that, do I?" Not the smooth introduction she'd planned. "He's coming, isn't he?" *So much hinges on this. Please tell me he'll be here any minute.*

"No." He took another sip of his coffee and made room for the server to set down his meal order, and a duplicate of the plate in front of Alexis.

Quiche. The man eats quiche.

"My dad is unavoidably detained."

Oh, no.

"For the next three or four weeks. Maybe six."

"What? What are you saying?" The production schedule couldn't afford a three-*day* delay, much less three weeks.

He sat with his head bowed a moment, then said, "Blew out a disc in his back last night loading camera equipment into the van. We didn't know how bad it was until he called from the medical center an hour ago." He spread what looked like blackberry jam on the rustic toast that came with their quiche. "They're still deciding whether to do surgery or not. But in any case, he's unavailable for a while. I'm Gabe, by the way."

"I'm devastated. Pleased to meet you." As good as it smelled, breakfast would not sit well in her stomach. Ever again. *Yes, Aunt Sarah, I came by the title Drama Queen honestly. I earned it.*

"Well, Devastated, I hope you don't mind choosing a new nickname. I'm here to fill in for my dad."

"I know you meant that to sound comforting, but—" She

got as far as picking up her fork. No further. Her mind raced ahead to the disastrous possibilities. George Langley came with credentials and videography awards. Gabe Langley came with . . . jam on his shirt. "You have a little something right"—she pointed to the spot—"there."

"Now, see? If I'd worn my flannel lumberjack shirt, it would have blended right in." He swiped at the dark blob with his napkin.

Flannel. Lumberjack.

"Miss Blake . . . "

"Alexis."

That irritatingly bright smile stole across his face again. "Let me assure you I've had more than a little experience behind a video camera. Hey, Kevin!"

From across the room, a young man with tasteful highlights and an unnatural tan waved back. "Gabe."

"Did I or did I not do a magnificent job filming your wedding this summer?"

"Magnificent. As of today, Melissa and I are still married."

"And there you go," Gabe said, as if that settled it. "Try the quiche. It's great."

The conversation had gone on too long. "Gabe, I appreciate your willingness to fill in for your dad. But I'm not sure you understand what's at stake."

"I think I have an idea. You're restoring an old house in the area and you need someone to film the process."

"Yes, but it's not just for my own use."

"I know that. I read the contract."

"Which your *father* was supposed to sign today."

The too-bright face darkened. "Miss Blake, I do know how to sign my name."

The sweater was a bad decision. Heat radiated underneath it and crept through the neck opening to her fevered cheeks. "Please don't think I'm dismissing your"—she glanced toward the happily married Kevin—"obvious talent. But I need a professional for this project. If it goes well, I have an opportunity to lock in a spot on next year's *Restoring Christmas* special on the Heart-and-Home Channel. Can you imagine what that could do for a designer's career? It could lead to my potentially having my own show. Me."

"And if it doesn't go well?"

Sure. Call me out on the risk I'm taking. That'll win points. "Then the costs incurred for the construction, decorating, filming, everything are my responsibility. And I'm back to being one of Chicago's least-known, least-experienced, no-name wannabes designing sunrooms and the occasional bathroom makeover. 'Would you like polished chrome or nickel faucets on your soaker tub?'"

"Oil-rubbed bronze. But that's just me." He opened the flap on a leather pouch leaning against the table leg between them. "Does this put your mind at ease?"

His business card? Anyone could print a decent-looking business card.

"Read the fine print," he said, then looked away, as if embarrassed that he'd asked it of her.

"You won a Telly Award?"

"Two. I didn't want to brag, so I . . . just said 'Telly Award winner.' Besides, 'two-time Telly Award winner' would make the card look . . . crowded. Don't you think? From a design perspective?"

What option did she have? The man with jam-stain on his long-sleeved T-shirt or give up the dream. She'd be hard-pressed to find a replacement willing to devote eight weeks of long days working for half the normal fee but the "potential" promise of industry recognition if Alexis's project won the slot on *Restoring Christmas*.

It was Gabe, offspring of the man she wanted to hire, or nothing.

"Your name wasn't on the company website."

"My dad's the genius," he said, pushing the last bite of crust to the side of his plate. "I'm merely the undergenius."

"You'll have to work on your self-esteem issues, Mr. Langley." She teased her food with the tip of her fork.

"It's a tax liability issue. And I'm okay with that. Until my dad retires and the business is turned over to me—if I keep my nose clean, so to speak—I work for him. Humbling, but good. I couldn't ask for a better boss."

They ate in silence, reserving their comments to the food.

How would Gabe Langley feel having *her* for a boss? *One*

way to find out. "When you're done, let's go meet the home owner, then."

"That wasn't too painful, was it?"

"Yet to be determined." Alexis pushed away from the table and snagged her coat from the back of the chair.

"Do you want a to-go box for that?" As he stood, he pointed to her uneaten breakfast.

"No. I haven't checked in yet, so I don't know if my room has a fridge and microwave."

He helped her into her coat. "Where are you staying?"

"Shoreview? Bayview? Lakeview. Something like that."

"You just listed the names of most of the motels within a hundred miles of here." His laughter sounded like a comedian's favorite audience member. Loud. Strong. Genuine.

"What projects won you a Telly?"

He held the door for her and waited while she pulled on her gloves. "A couple of commercials I did for cable TV."

"What were they about?"

"You don't want to know."

"I think I do."

"Which direction is your car?" he asked.

"I parked on the street."

He hesitated. "I'm around back."

A muscle at the base of her neck tightened. "Gabe, what were your Telly Award–winning commercials?"

"Pat's Pond Scum Protection."

What could she read in the tilt of his eyebrows? Was he

joking again? "No. Really." Any miniscule calm she'd retrieved scooted out of reach.

He punched a button on his key fob. A faint beep signaled he'd successfully unlocked his vehicle. "Really. Pond Scum Protection."

"Well, then . . . "

Eight weeks until the final scene at Christmas. Eight weeks that had seemed so short earlier that morning now stretched light-years into her shaky future.

CHAPTER TWO

"THAT'S *IT*?" GABE SLAMMED THE DOOR of his van and joined her on the gravel at the gap in the low-slung fieldstone fence at the front edge of the property.

"Don't say it like that."

"Like what?"

"I think it's charming." Alexis took a picture of the scene with her cell phone. Then another.

Gabe lifted his video camera to his right shoulder. "Didn't say it wasn't. You might want to"—he reached with his left hand to smooth her hair.

"You're filming already?"

"Initial reaction footage. Act natural. And don't look at me. I'm invisible."

If only. "Gabe, we haven't talked about the video style I'm looking for, the kind of footage that will be useful, the parameters the Heart-and-Home executives laid down for this project . . ."

"Take a few steps up the driveway."

"Gabe."

"Wasting good light here."

Something told her she would be a well-practiced *sigh*-er before this was all over.

"Keep walking, Alexis. That's good. It looks like you're a prodigal daughter returning home."

She glared at him over her shoulder.

"Try that again, but without the attitude."

Eight weeks. Eight long weeks. Some counted the days until Christmas with sweet little advent calendars. Alexis would count them by numbers of fried nerve endings.

She turned to face the house again, a long driveway and a meandering creek between her and her architectural and design challenge. The photos she'd seen hadn't been able to capture the way the house seemed both lonely and inviting at the same time. Two-story fieldstone that showed age and strength in one package. Low porch roof indicated lower ceilings inside than most modern construction. An opening in the stone foundation led, no doubt, to a stone-cold cellar. And an off-center front door mimicked the front elevation on the second floor. Three windows, unevenly spaced, rather than the symmetry expected from mid-American farmhouses. One window was missing a shutter. Already on her task list for the construction team.

"Do you think that bridge will hold more than a horse-drawn carriage?" Gabe stood at her side, his camera lens sweeping the landscape.

"I imagine it can," Alexis said, "since that's probably how

the owner got her SUV across the creek." She tapped him on the shoulder and pointed toward the vehicle hiding all but its backside behind the house. "Not exactly what I expected a woman in her seventies would drive."

"As opposed," Gabe said, "to the woman in her—late twenties . . . ?" He focused the lens on her face.

"Close enough." Both his estimate and his nearness.

" . . . who drives *that* sweet ride." He panned behind them to her pumpkin spice sedan.

"My Aunt Sarah's. She claims she ordered the metallic copper."

Gabe's head emerged from behind the camera. "Yeah, that's not copper. Or metallic."

"We know. My BMW is in for repairs. What? You doubt I drive a BMW?"

"No." His eyes danced. "I'm surprised a BMW needs repairs."

Alexis drew a full-lung breath. "So that three-week thing for your dad is nonnegotiable, right?"

"Alexis . . . " He turned his attention away from her. Was he more sensitive than she thought?

"I apologize. I'm a little on edge, considering what's at stake for me." She hugged her coat tighter around her.

"Can you imagine how she feels?"

"Who?" Alexis followed the path of his gaze.

"The woman staring at us from the porch."

A quick breath this time. "That must be Elsie."

"Lick your lips."

"I beg your pardon?"

"Capturing the moment the designer meets the home owner. And . . . action!"

"MRS. RAYMOND . . . it's such a pleasure . . . to finally . . . meet you."

"You don't work out much, do you? That little walk up the driveway made you breathless, did it?" The slight woman, dressed in a puffy quilted vest that might have kept her warm but accentuated her too-thin arms, pursed her lips as if tasting raw rhubarb for the first time.

Maybe instead of auditioning for the *Restoring Christmas* special, Alexis should shift gears and work on a *Peace on Earth* special. "I'm . . . we were in a hurry to meet you. This is Gabe Langley, the videographer."

He waved from behind the camera.

"Best get your vehicles off the road—that autumn mist thing and the utility van," the woman said. "You're blocking traffic."

Traffic? They hadn't heard or seen any other vehicles on the side road since they'd arrived. And it was clearly pumpkin spice, not autumn mist. "We'll do that. Is there room enough to park behind the house?"

"I should hope so." Elsie crammed her hands into her vest pockets. "Watch for the chickens. That's all I ask."

They headed back down the driveway and across the bridge. Silent for the first hundred feet.

Gabe cleared his throat. "We may need to do some careful editing on that segment."

"We may wind up with *no* usable footage by Christmas Eve." The truth of her statement made her mouth go dry.

He laughed. "Oh, ye of little faith."

"Oh, ye of too much."

"Enough to know this will be an adventure. I'm up for it. Are you saying you're not?"

She let his words hang unanswered and sought temporary solace behind the wheel of her "sweet ride." It needed cinnamon. And whipped cream. And she needed a crash course in patience.

Alexis knew better than to convert that need into a prayer. Who knew how God might choose to answer that one? He'd apparently thought Gabe Langley fit into the category of Answers to Prayer.

The Curiosity in the van behind her backed up so she had room to maneuver through the opening in the fieldstone fence and lead the charge up the hill to Elsie's place, Alexis's project. Alexis's expanding predicament.

"You can come through here," Elsie called as they exited their vehicles. Even from that distance, the deteriorating back door she held open found a spot on Alexis's to-do list.

"Leave the camera equipment in the van for this first visit, Gabe. She might feel more comfortable."

"Got it, boss."

Yes. It was possible to mentally roll your eyes without physically rolling them.

"Hey, boss?" Gabe stood motionless.

"Hmm?"

"Is that a . . . a working outhouse?"

Alexis glanced at the wood and stone structure tucked among the trees at the edge of the backyard. "No. That's the chicken coop."

"Oh."

She heard the relief in his voice. "*That's* the outhouse." She nodded toward a near twin of the first structure. "Notice the well-worn path?"

"You're okay with that?" he whispered as they neared the back door.

"Top of my list, Mr. Langley. Top of the list."

Elsie Raymond ushered the two through a narrow back entry lined with an assortment of boots and shoes. "Hang your coats here, if you want."

They found empty hooks along one wall and followed Elsie into her kitchen.

"I made tea." She spoke the words as if daring them to say they didn't like tea.

"Tea sounds great," Alexis said. She eyed Gabe. They chose two of the ladder-back chairs tucked around a square table in the middle of the larger-than-expected but sparsely furnished room.

"Love a good cup of tea," Gabe agreed. His height and bulk—not pudginess, definitely not—more than filled the chair.

"Didn't say it was good." The corners of Elsie's lips curled upward. She had a sense of humor after all. The woman poured from a red enamel teapot with a sturdy black handle and filled three matching red mugs before sitting. "I have sugar, if you want it. But I'd have to get up for it."

"I can get it." Gabe stood, the legs of his chair scraping against the hardwood floor. "Where?" He found the sugar canister and pulled open drawers until he found spoons.

Alexis caught Elsie's amusement.

"You going to need that much, young man? I do have a sugar bowl there on the counter."

Gabe smiled. "I might need more than one cup of tea."

Elsie nodded. "Well, then . . . " Her sentence led nowhere. Until, "My father used honey in his tea. When he . . . lived with me."

Alexis experimented with several opening phrases in her mind. None sounded like a professional introduction to the discussion they needed to have. So she settled for, "I appreciate your willingness to participate in this *Restoring Christmas* project, Mrs. Raymond."

"Elsie. Might as well call me Elsie."

"How did you first connect with the Heart-and-Home production team? I wasn't told how you and your house were chosen."

Elsie sipped her tea. "A friend of mine entered my name in their contest. She took pictures when I was getting something out of the garden. Sent them in without my knowing."

Gabe stirred his tea. "Is she still your friend?"

"Gabe!" Alexis was going to have to start looking for another videographer. Maybe Sturgeon Bay had someone. Or Green Bay. The distance wasn't that much different. Mileage costs would kill the budget, but . . .

"It's a fair question, Alexis." Elsie smoothed her hands over the tabletop as if she could feel its wrinkles with her own. "I kept her as a friend. I just don't talk to her much anymore. She feeds the animals when I'm gone."

"Aren't you excited about the prospects of having your home brought more up to date, get a few repairs taken care of, and have it professionally decorated for the holidays?" Alexis watched Elsie's face for a hint of enthusiasm.

"I don't mind the repairs. But this"—she lifted the handle on the red teapot—"is about all the decorating I've done for Christmas since I moved here. Ever since my boys—" She pursed her lips again. "Don't do much entertaining for Christmas."

"Maybe you will this year." Alexis looked to Gabe for backup.

"Are you sure you're comfortable with having us invade your house like this, Mrs. Raymond? Miss Blake, me, the construction crew . . . "

Big help. Big, big help, Gabe.

Elsie pursed her lips, the action deepening the lines around her mouth. "I wasn't expecting to be comfortable with it. But it needs doing. I have to do it."

"I can't pretend it won't be interruptive, Elsie." Alexis laid her hand over Elsie's. "But we'll do our best to keep things from getting too chaotic. Are you sure you don't want to take the network up on its offer to pay for a motel or send you to stay with a family member until we're done with the messy jobs?"

Elsie slid her hand from underneath Alexis's. Her posture stiffened. "I have to be here. To supervise."

"That's kind of my job," Alexis said.

"And who else but me will supervise you?"

CHAPTER THREE

"She must have used up her quota of gratitude for the month." Alexis stared at her phone, but it offered no comfort.

"Sounds as if Elsie hasn't had the easiest life."

Where had he gotten that? The woman had been offered a sweet, no-cost-to-her home renovation. Anyone else would have been falling all over themselves with joy, wouldn't they? "I guess I expected I'd be working with someone who knew how to show a little enthusiasm."

Gabe mimed a running back's touchdown celebration.

"Not you." She shook her head. "The home owner."

"It wasn't her idea in the first place. Sounds like she hasn't yet warmed to it."

"But still . . . "

"Problem? I mean, other than that slightly outdated—and long distance—version of an en suite bathroom?" Gabe pinched his nose, a visual *Eww*.

Their footsteps crunched on the leaf-strewn gravel behind the house as they headed for their vehicles and the next step. Alexis stopped. What was her next step? So far she had an uncooperative client, an overly exuberant videographer replacement, and a challenge that had been daunting before either of those two had even entered the picture. To say nothing of the persistence of Christmas waiting for its cue, whether she was ready for it or not.

"Problem? No. Nothing I can't handle." Alexis did resort to prayer then. *Lord, don't make me eat those words.*

WITHIN MINUTES they were a two-vehicle caravan on County Highway S again, aptly named Lakeview Drive, tracing the curve of the shore that angled southwest to head the several miles back into Algoma. They drove past the marina and over the bridge on the Ahnapee River, or An-Ne-Pe, in the language of the original Potawatomi. She hadn't gotten far enough in her research yet, but knew that much. Algoma had once been called Wolf River because of the An-Ne-Pe—Great Gray Wolf—flowing through it.

"Do you ever feel inadequate, little river—so close to the real attraction, the Lake Michigan water that can be seen from outer space?" She stayed close enough behind the white van so she wouldn't lose Gabe as they wound their way through town. Her laptop bag, bulging with plans and dreams, slid across the passenger seat when Gabe signaled and took an abrupt right.

Not the direct route to the Crescent Beach boardwalk. She knew that much. At random intervals, he braked, stuck his arm out the driver's side window, and pointed at something. His version of a guided tour? If she knew the significance of what she was seeing, his arm might have been more appreciated.

Residential districts. A mix of historic homes and not-so-historic. Tree-shaded streets . . . or they would have been if the leaves weren't gone from most of the trees already. Everywhere reminders that autumn was breathing its last gasps, about to turn the keys over to a northland winter. Corn shocks. Typical Halloween yard decorations. And pumpkins the color of . . . the car she was driving.

The white van led at last to a narrow parking lot shimmed between Lake Street and the water's edge at the base of the rock-and-cement breakwater that stretched out into Lake Michigan. Standing sentinel at the breakwater's tip, Algoma's rocket-shaped red lighthouse.

Even before she exited the car, the lighthouse made its presence clear. It reminded her of a Buckingham Palace guard in its red coat. Unwaveringly at attention. Unmoved by the pounding waves or the riot of water birds coming and going. Unaffected by the jeers of the seagulls, squawking and stripping fish skeletons at its feet.

"Impressive, isn't it?" Gabe had her door open before she finished unbuckling her seat belt. "Do you have a hat? You'll need it. The wind."

"This is a bad time for sightseeing, Mr. Langley. Sure, we

need some footage of the locale, the hometown flavor. But I have a few trillion details to take care of. And I have yet to check into the hotel that will be my home for the next two months." If she could have written how this assignment would start, her version would bear little resemblance to what had transpired since breakfast at Caffé Tlazo.

"All the more reason to ponder. I do my best pondering here. Board meetings, I call them. Time for a *Restoring Christmas* board meeting, don't you think? So we're on the same page?" He started toward the curb-like wall at the south edge of the parking area, with the boardwalk beyond it.

"You're not bringing your camera?" She hustled to keep up with his long strides. The scene would make great footage. The curve of the beach. The benches at intervals. The sand and water and . . . What was that? Seagull droppings.

"The light's gone flat on us."

So it had.

When his feet hit the boardwalk, his pace decreased dramatically.

"I can keep up," she said.

"It's not that. The faster we walk, the faster our brains whirr."

"Sounds like exactly what I—"

"The opposite of what you need right now."

He walked on her right so as not to "block her view." Kind of him. But he wasn't blocking her from the wind either. It raced across the churning water and found the spaces between the tight threads of her coat. Considerable cooldown since earlier in the day. And it wasn't even noon. Was it? That meant she had at least three hours to kill before she could check in at her motel. Maybe she could work at the coffee place for a while.

They'd reached a spot in the boardwalk where a side branch led to easy beach access. Gabe gravitated that direction. She followed. The initial stretch of pebbles was like walking in a pan of marbles. The deep, soft sand also challenged her ability to walk upright. As they neared the water's edge, the sand grew damp and firm.

"These waves are unpredictable," Gabe said, tugging on her sleeve until she retreated farther back from the place where the sea and land met. Moments later, her fresh footprints disappeared under a water hand.

He bent at the waist. "Here. You might like this."

"What is it?" She held her gloved palm open.

"A rock shaped like a heart. My mom used to collect them." He looked far up the beach. "I got her collection when she died."

"How long ago?" Alexis fingered the smooth contours of the slate-gray stone.

"A year this December."

Her throat tightened as it always did when confronted with someone's loss. "That's harsh."

"Hard," he said. "Not harsh. A lot of good memories, even in the months after they discovered the tumors."

"Months?"

"I've often wondered . . . "

She shouldn't pry. She had to. "What? You've wondered what?"

He took a deep breath and arched his shoulders. "I've wondered which would have been worse—losing her so fast the way we did, or watching her suffer longer."

Gabe, there's a lot more to you than . . . than . . . I can afford to think about right now. "You should keep this rock."

He stuffed his hands in his pockets. "I think you probably need it."

"Need it? Long walks on the beach, and all that?"

His pinched brow told her she might have misinterpreted the gesture.

"I thought you might need a reminder that the same waves that crash against the shore also create art out of stone. Fieldstone. Elsie's house. Your project. Get it?"

"Heart art?" She turned the stone in her hand.

He shrugged. "So, are we going to do this thing?"

Create heart art together? Uh . . . no. Definitely not, Gabe Langley.

"I may not be as experienced as the videographers you've worked with in the past. I can show you examples of my work, if that will help. Other than pond commercials and the occasional beach wedding. I have a portfolio. It's not extensive yet, but . . . "

"Nothing about this project is going to be easy, you realize." She'd watched his overconfidence fade into a paler version of itself. Flat light, as he said. But the look on his face said he wanted a chance to prove himself. *Alexis, it's not as if you have another option.*

"I suppose we all have something to prove, don't we?"

What did he mean by that? She wasn't about to unload her baggage to a replacement videographer with jam on his shirt and—

"Well." He started away from the water toward the boardwalk. "Either way, I'll help you with your baggage."

"What?"

"I'll help you get checked in and haul your luggage from your car." He glanced back at her. "Algoma is famous for a lot of things, but bellhops aren't among them."

Algoma . . . famous for . . . baggage . . . bellhops . . . He was concerned she wouldn't think him good enough to pull off the video gig? That he'd lose the contract, or rather, his dad's contract? Okay, she wasn't completely without her doubts, but he did not have a lock on insecurities. *Now, there's a powerhouse team for you. A woman who's banking her career on a renovation project for a home owner who doesn't want one, and a videographer with a point to prove and a collection of his mother's heart-shaped rocks.*

Funny. Those hadn't been details of any of her life's dreams.

"Let's do this," she said.

"Do you want references?"

"Do you have any?"

"My dad."

"Yeah." She stepped onto the boardwalk right after he did. "I don't think that will be necessary."

"Right after we sign the contract, I'll tell you about my criminal record." He sprinted ahead toward the parking lot.

CHAPTER FOUR

CRIMINAL RECORD. Good one. She caught up to Gabe midway back to the parking lot. "How do you know you can trust *me?* For all you know, I could be a drug dealer."

"I can recognize drug dealers. Don't ask how I know. It was a long time ago. Lifetime ago."

They'd almost reached the parking lot. He stopped and faced her. "Can you be trusted to be true to your word?"

"Of course."

"I believe you." He resumed walking.

"Gabe, that's crazy."

"Are you hungry?"

"Did you ask me that because my stomach growled?" She slapped her hand against its rumbling.

"No. Because of . . . wait for it." He held his phone toward her. "Twelve noon."

It had been too long since their last cup of tea with Elsie. But finding something to eat and drink didn't top her priority list. "I need a place to think more than I need to eat." *You said*

29

I could think while walking the boardwalk. But it brought more questions.

"They're not mutually exclusive activities, you know. Thinking and eating. I know a place. Follow me."

He knew a place. She'd tolerate him, because she hoped above hope Gabe also knew videography.

She followed the van, which took a less rambling route this time, ending in a subdivision on a hill above and to the north of the town's business district. A white ranch-style house with green shutters and an equally Christmas-green metal roof stared at her. Solid, but plain. Unblinking. Lousy location for a restaurant.

Gabe gestured for her to follow him through the door in the covered breezeway connecting the garage to the house. "Hey, Dad," Gabe called. "I'm home. And I have company."

Dad? That makes more sense. This is his father's house. But did we really need to stop here first?

"You'll have to come to me," a voice answered back. "Not moving from this spot."

They found Gabe's father, the man Alexis thought she'd be working with, silver hair, deep-water eyes, with his back pressed against the side of the refrigerator in the stuck-in-the-nineties kitchen.

"Are you Miss Blake?" he said, arms at his side, moving only his eyes.

She stepped in front of him. "I'm Alexis Blake, George.

Yes. Pleased to meet you." She retracted her hand when he made no attempt to shake it.

"Practicing your statue stealth maneuvers, Dad?" Gabe opened the fridge and withdrew bottled water for each of them.

"I can't find the heating pad," George said. "I've been icing my back, like the doctor said. But heat feels better. Old refrigerators like this one don't have as much insulation, so it gives off plenty of heat. Oof." He stepped away from the appliance. "The pain in my legs won't let me stand here long, though."

Gabe handed Alexis both her water and his own and rushed to help his dad shuffle his way to the couch across the open concept kitchen/family room. Once settled there, George waved off his son and addressed Alexis.

"I apologize for any inconvenience I've cost you. Please let me assure you that Gabe is no Plan B. He's a skilled videographer. I wouldn't have sent him to you if I didn't think so."

"Thanks, Dad." Gabe busied himself adjusting his father's pillows and straightening the collection of magazines and books on the coffee table near the couch. "I think the heating pad is in the hall closet. I'll look."

Seconds later Gabe returned with both the heating pad and an extension cord, which he wasted no time getting set up.

"Thanks, son. I miss you when you're not here."

It sounded like something her aunt Sarah would say to her. Had said to her. Alexis made a mental note to call her aunt and see if she'd have any free time after the holidays to reconnect. She couldn't afford the cross-country flight to Oregon often. But it was past time.

"Dad, I live downstairs."

Oh. No. A basement dweller.

"I know that look," Gabe said.

"What look?" Alexis reined in what must have shown in her facial expression.

"It's a nice apartment, and I could live on my own if I wanted to. Above ground, even." He mimicked the action of a groundhog digging its way to the surface, then poking its head out to see if the coast were clear.

The man clearly had issues.

Alexis stepped closer to Gabe's father. "George, it was a pleasure to meet you. I'm sorry we aren't getting an opportunity to work together. I was so impressed with what I saw on your website."

"Gabe did most of the website work. But, thank you."

He did? Maybe the son in this equation had played a larger part in Langley Videography than she gave him credit for. "I need to get to my motel and plow into a few adjustments to my plans now that I've seen the location for the project. So, if you'll excuse me . . . ? I hope your back heals quickly, George. Thank you, Gabe, for the introduction. And for stepping in."

"Looking forward to it," Gabe said. "Is that your phone?"

"I apologize for the annoying ringtone. Thought I had it muted." She walked through the door to the Langleys' breezeway as she answered. After the first few words of the conversation, she sank onto the rough bench along one short wall.

Why can't anything be easy?

HOW LONG HAD SHE been sitting there, staring at her phone, before Gabe opened the door and stepped into the breezeway? Five minutes? Ten?

"Your pumpkin won't start?" he asked.

"Oh, it had better."

"Great imitation of a snarling badger. Wisconsin's state animal. Wouldn't have been my top choice."

He sat on the bench beside her. The too-short bench.

"Trouble?"

"I got a phone call," she said, her voice a mirror of the stomach growl that accompanied her statement.

"I . . . do remember that." He propped one ankle over the opposite knee. "We were going to get some lunch. Stopped at Dad's. Phone call. And, yes. Up to speed."

He'd wait forever if she didn't tell him the story, not that it was any of his business.

"Tell me," Gabe said. "Can't be that bad."

"My motel was skunked."

Saying the words didn't make them believable. *Skunked?*

Gabe uncrossed his legs. "This time of year?"

"So, there's a proper time of year to skunk a motel?" *The man has no sympathy.*

"I just meant they're a lot more active in the spring, usually. How does an entire motel get—?"

She stopped his question with her raised hand. "Don't know how. As they say, 'It just *is*.'"

"What do you know? Skunk attack."

Unheated breezeway. She hadn't stopped to notice before now. "I guess I'll have to call around. Or drive around. The size of Algoma, that shouldn't take long."

"Extended stay? You might have a little difficulty finding a place for the full eight weeks."

"Why?"

"Kewaunee's Quilt and Artisan Festival spills over to Algoma's accommodations. We usually pick up quite a lot of the Door County need for housing for their fall activities. By the end of November, you're talking the start of Christmas events, too. The calendar's fuller than you might think up here on the edge of nowhere."

"I only need one room. With Wi-Fi. And maybe a fridge. And a microwave, if possible."

"At a reasonable price."

She sighed. "That, too. Ideas?"

Gabe spelled out the pros and cons of the town's and

surrounding area's harbor-/beach-/shore-/river-/water-view motels, making a point to remind her he couldn't guarantee any would have vacancies for the length of time she'd need a room.

"How long do you think it will take for the skunk smell to vacate my original choice?"

He chuckled. "Should be yet this century."

"Gabe!"

"It'll be a while. But all is not lost. We have options."

We *have nothing. I need options. And Christmas is going to come faster than any year in the prior history of the world.* "Like what?" *Alexis, what are you doing? You're soliciting counsel from a local you met a couple of hours ago. Listening to the advice of a football player–turned–videographer–turned–thorn in your side.*

"I know some people."

"Many a shady black-market deal has started with those four words." She shrugged her shoulders deeper into her coat.

"How do you feel about a yert?"

"Excuse me?"

"You know what a yert is, don't you?"

Blood pressure? A hundred and too much over too much. "I'm well aware. A glorified tent. With a wood floor. And odd-shaped walls impossible to accessorize. And outdoor plumbing. You do remember that I'm philosophically against outdoor plumbing in winter climates?"

"It was a joke. But I'm impressed. You've designed yerts?"

A gust of wind stole through the open-at-both-ends breezeway. "One. One yert. For school. And by 'design,' I mean interior design. I didn't build it."

"Might be an interesting challenge." His expression—as always—held a level of enthusiasm uncommon to men of his age and stature.

Blood pressure—danger level.

"But no. We don't have time for that," he said, as if rooting himself in reality. "You need a place to live."

"A place for tonight," she said. "I'll drive back to Green Bay, if I need to."

"Packer home game tonight. Nationally televised. You'd have to drive an hour beyond Green Bay to find a room."

"It's Thursday."

"Hence the addition of the word *televised.*"

A faint voice called through the door of the house proper. "Gabe? You there?"

Gabe stood. "Let me see what Dad needs. I'll be right back." His hand on the doorknob, he stopped. "That's crazy. Come on in from the cold while I see to Dad. I promised you lunch. We'll see what he has in the fridge. Are you into bologna sandwiches with stinky cheese?"

"Don't worry about me." She followed him into the house.

George lay on the couch—most of him—with one hand propped on the floor. "I've almost fallen and I can't get upright." His jungle-undergrowth eyebrows quirked at such a comical angle that Alexis had to stifle laughter.

"How did you get yourself into that pickle?" Gabe asked, bracing his dad under his arms and gentling him back into a safer position on the couch.

"Dropped my glass of water. Which is"—he pointed gingerly at the floor without moving his torso—"another bit of a problem."

Alexis grabbed paper towels from the kitchen and handed them off to Gabe.

"Dad, you may need—" His abrupt halt turned all eyes toward him.

George cringed. "A babysitter?"

"That's not what I was going to say. You may need more help than you're used to allowing. For a while."

"I could have figured this out, eventually. It's worse in the evenings. And if I have to get up in the middle of the night. The muscles in my back don't like the darkness, I guess. They throw a fit." He moved himself a little closer to the back of the couch and winced again.

Gabe retrieved the water glass and soggy paper towels and tore more from the roll. "It got me thinking. You, too, Alexis?"

"What?" *What am I supposed to be thinking?*

"It seems God knew about your need before the first skunk squirt."

I should leave town, turn around at the outskirts, come back, and start this day all over again. This alternate universe thing is creeping me out.

"I think our Miss Blake may be as confused by that

37

statement as I am, son. Not that I doubt the God part. Or that He knows about skunk squirt." George took the fresh bottled water—with a lid on it—that Alexis offered to him.

"Her motel needs a seagoing vessel full of deodorizer, Dad."

"Ah, musty, huh?" George nodded his head.

"A little more serious than that."

While Gabe explained and dug through George's refrigerator, Alexis stepped back to Google accommodations within twenty miles of Algoma. She clicked on the calendars on the most likely websites. Gabe hadn't been kidding. No rooms available for those dates popped up too often. She could see openings, but they dotted the calendar rather than ran in a nice, long, eight-week stretch. She switched gears and searched for something, anything with an opening for two or three nights, preferably not wildlife friendly. One lead. But the price would have blown too much of the budget.

"Dad, when did you last get groceries?"

"It's been . . . a while."

"You need to eat." Gabe closed the refrigerator door. "Which completely supports my point."

Alexis pocketed her phone. It clunked against the rock that lived there. "And your point is . . . ?"

"We have a perfect storm. And a perfect shelter from the storm. Dad, you could use some help. Alexis, you need a place to stay."

Caregiving. For a stranger. While engaged in a consuming

*project that could rescue or destroy her career. Perfect storm, all
right.*

"I'll move up here with my dad and you can use my apartment downstairs." His self-assured grin—the Answer Man—seared her retinas. *How could he think—?*

"I told you my boy was smart." George's grin matched Gabe's. Although Gabe's had started to fade on the word *smart*.

Just when she was starting to trust the guy. A little. He thought she'd take him up on his offer? "Gabe, I'm not going to live in your apartment for the next eight weeks."

"Why not? It's a perfect solution. My dad can probably use my help while he's recovering, and you'll have a comfortable place to work and strategize and kick back. And you'll be able to save a little money in your production budget. It's only two months."

What was his definition of *comfortable?* And, for the record, there would be no *kicking back* until the video was done, edited, and sent to the Heart-and-Home producers. She stole a quick glance at him. What were the chances his apartment didn't smell like beef jerky and cheese puffs? Or worse.

It would not likely, however, smell like a family of skunks.

"So, Alexis is kind of in a bind. And you"—Gabe took a sip from his own bottle of water—"could use some extra help for a little while, couldn't you, Dad? Live-in help? I can't be around all the time, with the brutal work schedule Miss Blake will have for me, but I should be available most evenings."

He wouldn't have had to wink. The way he said *brutal* made it clear he was exaggerating.

You wouldn't have had to wink.

"And some days, she won't need me at all."

How does a person choke on water? She coughed her way back into reasonably proper breathing and said, "I'm not sure this is a good idea, Gabe. When you said you had an apartment—"

"I see where you're headed with this, son. And I think I agree with Miss Blake."

Finally. Someone speaking sense.

"She'd have to take a look at the apartment first, of course." Gabe shrugged out of his jacket and draped it over the arm of a well-worn chair. Then he reached for hers.

"I'll hang on to mine," she said. "I won't be here long." George Langley kept his house plenty warm, but Alexis needed the option of a quick getaway if things fell apart any more than they already had.

"If I were her," George said, bracing himself with his hands to shift his position, "I'd think you were a little bonkers to suggest such a thing . . . "

A man who understood.

" . . . without explaining our rental policy."

Who understood not enough.

"Our rental policy?" Gabe picked up the prescription bottle on the coffee table and raised his eyebrows as if checking for controlled substances.

"As I suspected. You didn't tell her, did you?" George instructed her to sit. A bird's-eye maple rocker beckoned.

"Dad, you don't charge me rent."

"Exactly. Are those terms acceptable to you, Miss Blake? Alexis?"

Alice Through the Looking Glass in a world where sharp lines were wavy and the only men she'd met so far shared a warped sense of humor. "Mr. Langley, I've barely started looking for another housing situation. This . . . crisis . . . is fresh. I'm sure I can find something if I have a little time to think"— she threw what she hoped was a piercing glance at Gabe— "and make some phone calls."

"Find something better than my basement?" He too looked at Gabe. Both men started laughing.

The theme song from *The Twilight Zone* flashed through her mind.

"Take her down to see it, Gabe. Put the poor woman's mind at ease."

This is how murder mysteries start. The seemingly kind young man and his invalid father suggest she go into their cobweb-draped basement. The gullible young woman complies, but at the top of the stairs, she realizes there are no lights, and a shove from behind pushes her into the dark abyss, where she languishes until she dies of starvation. Or worse.

Her stomach rumbled again. From the looks on their faces, it was loud enough for the whole room to hear. "That's really not necessary."

"Come on," Gabe said, that irrepressible smile doing a fine job of making him seem genuine. "There's an entrance to the basement apartment here"—he pointed as they passed a door near the breezeway connection—"but I usually leave that closed and use the outdoor entrance in order to respect Dad's privacy. Locks on both that one and this one, if you were wondering."

He led the way through the garage to another door near two wall-mounted bikes. "Here. Through here."

"You go first."

"As you wish." He unlocked the door, flipped a light switch, and descended the well-lit, plushly carpeted stairs ahead of her into the opposite of what she expected.

"Mom and Dad had started remodeling the place here, in the basement, with the intention of updating the upstairs, too, and getting it ready to sell so they could move to South Carolina. Dad can work anywhere. Mom was his business partner. And my sister's four kids . . . plus the weather . . . formed a strong pull. Anyway, this is as far as they got before Mom— Before her illness."

"I'm stunned."

"Kinda cool, isn't it?" He moved ahead of her, flicking on lamps and opening the honeycomb shades to reveal a wall of windows with a breathtaking view of the harbor, the lighthouse, and Crescent Beach. "I would have preferred hardwood," he said, "but my folks took great pains to muffle the noise between the two levels. They'd also considered spending summers here in this lower level and renting out the main floor all year around. After Mom died, I think Dad could consider either option."

Alexis took note of the tasteful décor, impeccable use of space, higher-end furniture choices. The fieldstone fireplace. Fieldstone. "It's gorgeous. And . . . tidy."

"You say that as if you're surprised I'm not a slob."

"It's this clean and you didn't know you'd have a visitor showing up?"

"You'll be grateful for that after you move in."

She scanned the kitchenette. Everything a person would need. Two-person table. Interesting blend of rustic and modern. Perfection. Except . . . "You have your Christmas tree decorated already?"

Gabe flipped a switch and undermount cabinet lights in the kitchen came to life. "I haven't taken it down from last year."

The month his mom died. How was he going to handle a video project with Christmas at its heart? Constant reminders.

"I'll need an hour or so to get my personal items hauled upstairs," Gabe said.

"Are you sure you don't need to talk this over with your father? Generosity is one thing, but your moving in with him . . . ?"

"He said you're an answer to prayer."

Sure, he did. Alexis couldn't help herself. She ran her hand over the satiny smooth surface of the console table behind the couch. "Is this Ranyae?"

"Hmm?" Gabe looked up from where he crouched near the bottom shelf of a storage cupboard. "Designer, you mean?"

"Yes."

"That's a Langley original."

"Father or son?"

"The . . . uh . . . son." He stood, an oversized duffel bag in hand. He set the bag on the round kitchen table and left the main area of the apartment, returning with an armful of clothing and toiletries.

"Gabe."

"Minute," he said, disappearing again.

"Gabe."

"Lunch is in the refrigerator. Leftover pizza." He stuck his head around the corner. "Do you mind warming it up? We have lots to talk about."

Time to regain control. "Gabe, I'm not staying here."

He emerged this time with an armful of sheets and pillowcases. "Laundry is under the stairs. Stackable washer and dryer. I'll be right back."

Pizza, huh? She opened the refrigerator door. Half a pizza. Enough for both of them. She located a nonstick frying pan and set it on the stove to heat. With the pan heated, she added the pizza slices.

"I figured you'd use the microwave," Gabe said.

"The crust crisps up this way." *He's doing laundry. I'm cooking. What's wrong with this picture?*

Everything.

"Paper plates okay with you?" he asked, opening a cupboard near her head.

Alexis pressed her hands to the base of her throat, doing her best to mimic a heart attack.

"That tacky, huh?" He slid the paper plates back where he'd found them.

"Kidding. Paper plates are fine for leftover pizza. But I need to make one thing clear."

"Yes, boss?"

She bit the inside of her bottom lip. Counted to five. Enough. "You're very kind."

"Thank you."

"I'm not done. You're very kind, but I can't evict you from your apartment."

He picked a piece of sausage from the pizza. "I wouldn't let you. I'm not being evicted. I'm emigrating upstairs." He held his right palm against his heart and raised his left hand. "'Give me your tired, your poor, your huddled masses longing to go help their dads recover from back injuries.' Emigrating, Alexis. It's the American dream."

She added her upper lip to her teeth sandwich, mostly to keep from laughing.

CHAPTER FIVE

"I'LL LEAVE YOU TO IT, THEN." Gabe hoisted the long strap of his duffel bag over his shoulder.

"You've decided I'm staying?" Alexis tossed the paper plates into the wastebasket she found under the sink. "Shouldn't it be my decision?" *Careful. Ingratitude is unbecoming, Alexis.* She could feel her aunt's counsel in her chest. Pulsing.

What hurt puppy could pull off a hurt-puppy look better than Gabe Langley? His expression soon righted itself to normal—calm, confident, but slightly mischievous. "Either way, I'm moving upstairs with Dad until he can get around better. It's the least I can do for him. If you don't *want* the apartment, the *rent-free* apartment I might add, that's up to you."

He grabbed a book from the console table behind the couch and headed for the stairs.

"You *know* this is . . . too perfect to pass up." She'd said it out loud without meaning to.

"I know that. The question is, do you?"

She could count on one hand the number of people she'd

been able to trust in her lifetime to date. Did Gabe Langley have no dark side? No foul history that would appear as soon as she let down her guard? Was his humor a cover? Or was it possible he was genuine? Goofy and irritating, but genuine. "Yes. I do know it's too perfect to pass up. For now. Thank you."

He took the stairs two at a time and called down, "Remember you said that."

Remember what? That she'd said *yes*? *Thank you*? Or . . . *I do*?

Don't get any ideas, Gabe. I am here for eight weeks only. And the project only. You are a coworker on this project.

And maybe a tiny bit of a distraction.

Alexis stood a long time at the window, enchanted with the view and the mesmerizing waves so like those that battered the Navy Pier in Chicago, yet somehow different. A tap sounded on the door at the top of the stairs.

And . . . it starts. He says he won't be an intrusion, and that I won't interrupt normal life for Gabe and his father. It starts already. She climbed halfway up the stairs, then stopped and said, "Yes?"

"Candygram."

"What?"

"Land shark."

She closed the gap and opened the door. "Not funny, Gabe."

He stood in the doorway with two of her suitcases.

"Brought these in from your pumpkin coach. I mean, your car. The rest is in the dumbwaiter."

She'd left her car unlocked. Not her norm. "You have a dumbwaiter?"

He skirted past her and hauled the luggage downstairs. "We thought it might help my folks in their retirement years if they chose the summers-in-Algoma option. Groceries. Garbage. Stuff like that. Oh, garbage day is every other Tuesday, just so you know." He deposited the bags in the bedroom Alexis hadn't entered yet.

They have a dumbwaiter.

"Well, I don't know about you, but I have work to do. I assume we'll start full-force in the morning?" He brushed his hands as if his job of righting all the wrongs of the world were done.

She nodded. "First thing in the morning."

"If you want to map out more details about the camera angles you want, lighting, the must-have scenes, we could do that over breakfast at Caffé Tlazo."

"I can make my own breakfast."

"So can I. It's just not as much fun. And"—he turned at the base of the stairs—"if we're going to use that time to plan out camera angles, we'd have to be *to-ge-ther*. Should we ride together? If so, it'll have to be the non-vegetable vehicle."

"What?"

"Not a pumpkin. The van. All my equipment is in there.

48

You'll need something bigger than a vegetable for hauling furniture and décor stuff, won't you?"

Décor *stuff?* Charming. "Most will be delivered to the fieldstone house. Elsie has an outbuilding—a shed—that has room for a lot of it. But yes, it would be helpful to have more space. Once in a while. It will also be helpful to have freedom to come and go as I need to."

"What would I be filming without you there, boss?"

She mimicked his smile. "Good point."

"What time should we leave?"

"I told Elsie we'd be there at nine. She's an early riser, but says she has enough chores to occupy her until close to nine."

"The chickens. As in, 'Up with the chickens.'" He stuck his hands under his arms and mimicked chicken wings.

Alexis, you have a choice here. Go along with him for once, or stick to your all-business-all-the-time self. "It's only logical," she said. "*Up*. Chickens."

"Logical?"

"*Down* comes from geese." She kicked off her shoes. Might as well, if she was staying. "See you at seven-thirty in the morning, then? Top of the stairs?"

His pause gave her confidence a boost. She was back in control.

"Good. Great. See you then," he said. "Don't forget your things in the dumbwaiter."

"Which would be . . . "

"Looks like a pantry door. Push the Down button and it will come . . . "

" . . . down?"

"Yeah."

"And the Up button here is to make it go . . . ?"

"Up." He quirked an eyebrow. "I guess it was self-explanatory."

"So it was. But thanks anyway. Really. Thanks for this temporary solution to my housing problem. I'll find another place soon."

She might have been mistaken, but she thought she heard him say, "Sure you will," as he ascended the stairs.

ON THE NEAR SIDE of the end of October. Alexis had been immersed in thoughts of Christmas for months already in preparation for the Heart-and-Home Channel project. She didn't dare think about the two other contestants vying for the same slot on the *Restoring Christmas* special—relative un-knowns, like herself, but designers whose body of work and interviews had risen above the hundreds of other applicants.

She massaged the back of her neck, admitting that part of the tension she felt on the project stemmed from her assumption that any day she'd receive a call from the producers letting her know there'd been a terrible miscalculation of votes. She was among the bottom three, not the top.

Curiosity might have killed the cat, but self-doubt can

paralyze a designer. The warning from one of her first semes-
ter instructors looped through her brain. How had he known
she'd need the truth embedded in her memory so it would
come to mind automatically at times like this?

Her design plans for the Christmas decorating segment
of the assignment could move only so far until she'd finalized
and gotten Elsie's approval for the structural changes. Making
the living space seem more open and inviting kept bumping
up against the significant need to find room for at least one
indoor bathroom. Preferably two. One upstairs, one down.

Resale value, Elsie. She'd have to pull that card a few times.
At seventy-two, how could Elsie not be motivated to consider
resale value when she eventually needed to sell or pass the
property to her—

Did Elsie have family? She'd mentioned sons. Yes.

Alexis made herself another cup of tea and jotted a note to
get groceries the next day, enough to last the week and replace
what she'd already used of Gabe's supply.

*You can tell a lot about a guy from what's in his fridge and
his pantry.* No generic tea. The high-quality kind she'd grown
to love in design school for its smoothness and staying power.
Balsamic reduction sauce. *Interesting.* A jar of pesto. A bag of
tortillas that looked homemade. *Hand*made. *Even more interesting.* Few pre-packaged foods. Mostly ingredients. A bowl of
fresh fruit on the counter. A well-stocked veggie drawer in the
refrigerator. High-end knife set. Artichoke hearts.

"If he cooks, get his number," Aunt Sarah often said.

I already have his number. And his wireless password. Aunt Sarah would be so proud.

Alexis had texted Gabe three times already since he'd relocated upstairs.

Wireless password?

Remind me to get a key from you in the morning.

Can I turn off the washer/dryer beeper? Quiet down here. Peaceful. Until it went off. Dug my claws into ceiling.

Her last question was met with his string of LOL's. He'd texted her twice more.

Dad wants my killer chili for supper. Send some up, please? In freezer. Glass container. (It eats through plastic.)

Feel free to have that for your own supper, too, if you want. Supposed to get cold tonight.

A quart jar of chili made its journey in the dumbwaiter from the basement apartment to the second floor. A pint jar of killer chili sat in the draining rack of the sink, thawing. Spicy didn't scare her.

Apparently, her fears were reserved for dryer beeping and what stared at her from the computer screen.

She wouldn't have chosen this career path if challenges scared her. Other than the challenge of never really knowing her parents—not in a healthy state. But her parents' choices had brought her Aunt Sarah, the life-changer. So, even that . . .

Challenges. Alexis didn't shy away from them. But Elsie's house could be her undoing. The mockup of the front elevation of the home—that fieldstone farmhouse from an era long gone—didn't offer the mental stressors the interior did. New exterior doors—not a problem. Replace the missing shutter and repair the one that hung crooked—simple task. Replace or reinforce the columns propping up the front porch. Paint the porch floor—a day's effort at the most.

She moved outdoor painting projects to the top of the tasks list, right behind demolition, depending on the weather. Forecasters predicted Indian summer within the next week. She needed at least fifty-degree temps for a string of days to guarantee the paint would dry properly.

Everything hinged on every other thing. Supply orders. Construction workers and their speed. And skill. The weather. Gabe. And none of it would matter if she couldn't come up with a workable plan for the interior.

She adjusted the floor plan of the home to the new measurements she and Gabe had taken during the morning's short visit. Alexis tamped down her disappointment-bordering-on-frustration that Elsie had "someplace she had to be" this afternoon, preventing a deeper investigation onsite. The home owner had agreed to the contest rules, which included remaining available for whatever the designer needed from her. Yet Day One, the long-retired woman had an afternoon appointment she couldn't miss?

Reluctant, reserved, disappearing client. Every designer's dream.

"God, all I want for Christmas is to win that spot on *Restoring Christmas.*"

The final words of her prayer hadn't stopped ringing before she realized that was like asking for world peace.

Including Korea.

SHE COULDN'T SLEEP. Not because of the killer chili. Maybe a little because of that.

More of her restlessness lay in her mind, not her stomach. Alexis opened her eyes and sat upright on the couch, the comforter from the bed wrapped around her like a shawl. Moonlight made the lifeless tree in the corner, decorated but unlit, more forlorn-looking than ever. A year since Gabe's mom's diagnosis. Almost a year since her death. It helped to have a sensitive, detail-oriented cameraman, but she couldn't afford an emotional basket case for a coworker. Did he regret leaving the memorial Christmas tree in the apartment? Should she haul it to the breezeway?

No. She couldn't keep him out of his apartment the whole eight weeks. She'd have to find some other arrangement. Although—sad unlit Christmas tree and all—this apartment really was ideal for her. Quiet. Private. Maybe what she'd save on housing fees would enable her to get a higher-end granite for Elsie's kitchen island and the pendant lights she'd had her heart set on since she saw them online the day she'd started dreaming.

She adjusted the comforter and padded to the tree corner. A mix of modern and antique ornaments. His mom's or grandmother's collection? The moonlight made some sparkle. Others remained shrouded in darkness, their features murky.

Her hand reached for the cord to plug the piggy-backed strings of lights into the wall socket. No. She shouldn't disturb Gabe's tribute to his mom, even if she touched nothing except the cord that could bring it to light. To life.

What did he expect to do? Light the tree on the anniversary of his mother's death? Wait and light it on Christmas Eve? Or had Alexis's presence messed up that, too.

You didn't mess up your parents' lives, Alexis. Aunt Sarah's voice filled the hollow spaces within her. *They self-destructed. It's because they loved you that they asked me to take you in until they got their heads straight.*

I was less than two years old when it started. Wasn't I reason enough for them to pull it together? Wasn't I enough?

Aunt Sarah had responded the same way every time Alexis asked that question. When Alexis was five and twelve and eighteen and a few weeks ago. She'd draw Alexis into her embrace and whisper, "And how sorry would my life have been if I hadn't had you in it?"

Alexis knew the kind of love that motivated Gabe to keep an unlit Christmas tree in his apartment and heart-shaped stones on his mantel. If it were her, she'd have two trees—one left dark, the other ablaze with the light and grace her aunt had poured into her. And still did.

She crossed the room and opened her laptop. After midnight. Her aunt wouldn't be on social media at this hour. Alexis composed a message that her aunt would find waiting for her in the morning. One more of a thousand gratitudes.

Gabe Langley seemed like the kind of guy to use social media. She typed his name into the search box. Gabe Langley, Algoma, Wisconsin. *Click*. Recent posts?

"Met a fascinating woman today."

Elsie. For all her reticence, Elsie harbored a lifetime of stories in her seventy-two-year-old body and mind. Her pale blue—chalk-blue—eyes hinted at stories they might never hear.

"Brilliant. Quick wit."

A sense of humor? Elsie? Alexis hadn't seen much of that yet. She kept reading.

"I'm looking forward to working with her on this project, trying to capture it through her viewpoint. What does she see when she looks at life through sapphire eyes?"

Elsie's eyes are— Oh.

Alexis rubbed her sapphire eyes and reread the post.

CHAPTER SIX

"GOOD MORNING, YOUNG ONES. Have you eaten?" Clad in knee-high rubber work boots, baggy jeans, and a camel-colored work coat with a corduroy collar, Elsie held an egg basket in one hand.

"We ate in town," Alexis told her as she ran ahead to get the back door for Elsie.

"Just as well. I got a late start."

Alexis followed her into the house. Gabe had ducked into the van for yet more camera and lighting equipment. "How was your doctor's appointment yesterday, Elsie?"

"Didn't say it was a doctor I saw."

"Oh." *What kind of appointment would have been serious enough to rearrange our schedules?*

"Strudel?"

"Excuse me?"

"Would you like a piece of cherry strudel?" Elsie asked, enunciating as if Alexis was hard of hearing.

"Is that what smells so good?"

Elsie slipped out of her boots and coat and carried the basket of eggs to the kitchen. She set it on the counter, rolled up her flannel sleeves, and washed her hands at the kitchen sink. The smell of sturdy soap made its contribution to the collection of aromas.

"Elsie. You have running water. Do you have a septic system on the property?" That would save Alexis thousands of dollars when installing the indoor bathroom.

"I do."

"But no indoor toilet."

"Seemed wasteful and unnecessary . . . when I was younger."

Could life be looking up? If the septic system was already installed . . .

"Sit. My dad's favorite breakfast treat. Or lunch. Or dinner. Or for no reason. Door County produces the best tart cherries for this. Handy to have them so close."

Cherry strudel. Perfect for the Christmas Eve scene. And with a story connected to it—her father. "I'd love a small sliver, please. No, that's too much. I don't—" She took the china plate Elsie offered. "That's perfect. Thank you."

Elsie cut a similar size for herself and one a little larger for the linebacker kicking a stainless-steel case across the floor in front of him as he entered the kitchen. His arms and shoulders were laden with an assortment of cameras, lens cases, stands, and two white hoops that looked like miniature trampolines.

"Why didn't you say something?" Alexis stood and helped Gabe divest himself of his burden. "I could have helped."

"You had your . . . purse," Gabe said, arching his back.

"Very funny."

"I could use an assistant, boss. Seriously. Working both the lighting and the camera is going to be tricky. And I can only do a stationary camera plus one roaming, so that'll mean—"

Elsie slid a plate closer to Alexis. "Offer him some cherry strudel. It has a calming effect," she said, her chalk-blue eyes twinkling this morning.

Gabe looked at Alexis, then at Elsie. "Did Alexis tell you we ate in town?"

"Yes, dear. She told me. Have some strudel."

Laughter tickled Alexis's throat. She kept her lips pressed together and turned her attention to the scenery beyond the kitchen window that faced the front yard.

"Good stuff," Gabe said.

"It was"—Alexis regained control—"her father's favorite when he was alive."

"Oh, he's still alive." Elsie poured herself a cup of coffee and slurped it noisily.

"He is?" Alexis could tell Gabe was calculating in his head, too. Elsie's dad had to be in his—

"He's ninety-three. I bought this place from him when it became obvious his mind was starting to go." Her jaw tightened visibly. "That went over well with my kids."

Elsie breathed deep as if needing a refill of oxygen to tell more of her story. "I took care of him until it was too much for me. He's in the Algoma Long-Term Care Unit in town.

I go see him twice a week, but it's been years since he knew who I am."

"I'm so sorry, Elsie." Maybe some of Elsie's brusqueness could be attributed to life's disappointments. Maybe she and Alexis had something in common after all.

"I'm sorry, too," Gabe said. He set down his strudel fork and gave the slight woman a hug.

Elsie fussed, and pushed him away. "It's part of life. I visit my father because *I* know who *he* is."

The light seemed different in the room. Hazy. Shadowed, though the sun shone bright. No house was without its pain. Even the irrepressible Gabe Langley's home. Was the loss of Elsie's dad's memories or the loss of his mother what she read in Gabe's eyes now?

Less than a year ago. In grief language, that meant it was sticky-fresh, still encased in the dampness of a monarch's wings.

She pinched her nose, high, near her tear ducts. Better. She could see more clearly now.

"You have plans to show me, Alexis?" Elsie slid the table's salt-and-pepper shaker centerpiece to the side.

Time to get real. More real. "Yes. I hope you'll like them." She opened her laptop and pulled up the files. She skidded her chair closer to Elsie so both could see the screen. Gabe had seen them at breakfast. He'd claimed he needed to "reserve" his comments until after Elsie had a chance to look at the plans.

"I started with the end product," Alexis said. "Then we'll peel back the layers until we get to the heart of where we have to begin in our renovation stage. Here you see the mockup of what your home will look like on Christmas Eve."

Elsie said nothing. She crossed her arms and leaned on the table, turning her head from side to side as if considering the flat picture on the screen from unseen angles.

"Elsie? What do you think?"

"It's . . . a lot."

"A lot to take in? Certainly. Most of my clients feel that way at first. Take your time. Would you like me to explain anything about what you're seeing on the screen?"

"It's . . . there's a lot of it."

"Modern doesn't have to mean minimalist," Alexis explained. "Notice how I incorporated both hard and soft edges with the metal sculptural pieces and the soft billows of fabric puddled at the windows and covering the wall behind the Christmas tree."

"Is that tree made of metal?" Elsie leaned closer.

"Copper. Isn't it stunning?"

The older woman leaned back. "How many copper kettles are you going to have to kill to make that thing?"

She doesn't like it? How can she not like it?

"Elsie," Gabe said, pulling his chair nearer, "no copper kettles will be harmed in the filming of this video." He thumped his fisted hand on his heart. "I'll personally guarantee it." Gabe winked at Alexis.

Not endearing. Not even a little.

She envisioned herself in Aunt Sarah's kitchen, her

legs—skinned knees and all—dangling a foot from the floor as she sat on the red vinyl stepstool seat, waiting to find out whether Aunt Sarah had finally decided soothing Neosporin could be as effective as the sting of Merthiolate.

Sting. Sting. Sting. Elsie didn't like the *signature* element of Alexis's design.

"I've put copper touches throughout the decorations, Elsie. Here, and here, on the side tables, the mantel. Let me show you the front elevation of the house. Then it will all make more sense to you." She scrolled through several frames. "Ah. See? Since we have to replace the porch roof anyway, I thought we'd go with copper. It'll shine like a . . . a . . . new penny. Okay, that's the only analogy I could think of at the moment. But it'll be gorgeous. Then, as it ages, it'll develop that stunning blue-green patina, which, as you can see, will then contrast with the chocolate color of the shutters."

"Not chocolate." Elsie's expression could have turned milk to buttermilk. Pure vinegar.

"They're beige now. They don't provide much contrast that way, though, Elsie. Here's the before and after of the front of the house. See?" Alexis flipped back and forth. *Before. After. Before. After.*

"The shutters were beige ever since we've been here."

"Consider for a moment how stunning the house could look if we chose a subtle contrast, like the one I'm suggesting. Help me out here, Gabe."

Gabe's smile flat-lined. "She wants them beige, Alexis. Maybe she's not into copper. And verdigris. And contrast."

"Thank you, young man." Elsie straightened and laid her hands in her lap. "I know you have all these wonderful ideas, Alexis. And you know more than I do about these things."

"Then"—Alexis searched for a kinder way to say what needed to be communicated—"will you trust me? It'll be beautiful."

"But it won't be me. Or mine. Or my father's legacy. And it won't be this house."

No wonder the producers didn't want us to meet our clients ahead of time. That would have been too easy. Let's up the tension by giving that Blake woman a client who wants nothing changed. "Every house can use improvement, Elsie. Even one as . . . sturdy as this one."

With her hands still in her lap, Elsie began to rock back and forth. Thinking? Fuming? "I don't mind changing some things."

"Well, good. That's a start."

"But some have to stay the same."

Alexis's sigh rustled the dusty curtain in the window.

Elsie's sigh beat hers both in velocity and endurance. "What's the name of that show you're trying to get on again? Are you going to *improve* on Christmas or *restore* it, Alexis?"

Maybe neither, if she couldn't get her client to cooperate.

ELSIE GAVE A NOD—close enough—to the small indoor bathroom tucked into the space near the back entrance. She agreed to indoor plumbing. Progress.

Financially, it wouldn't hurt Alexis to lose a few of the more extravagant details, but ordinary would not gain her the edge in the contest. And that was what mattered. Elsie might protest initially, but didn't most design clients? Even the celeb designers on the Heart-and-Home Channel ran into resistance. Their shows depended on it. Tension, tension, a disaster or two, an inevitable delay, and then . . . the reveal. Everybody's happy with how it turns out.

Elsie would come around.

"The work crew is coming in an hour to get started with demolition, Elsie. Can we at least agree on the open concept? We'll remove the wall between the kitchen and the great room. Basically, the whole downstairs becomes one open space."

"Seems unnatural."

Think fast. "Actually, some of the earliest settlements in this area probably had structures with one room that served as kitchen, eating area, living space, and even bedroom."

"You're talking one-room cottages?"

"You can think of it like that if you want."

"Built by those who emigrated here." Elsie's furrowed brow twisted into a shape more like considering. Thoughtful.

Was that the impetus Alexis needed? "What's your family's ancestry, Elsie?"

"Hmm?"

"I could tailor at least a few of the details in the *Restoring Christmas* remake of your home to your heritage. I assume Raymond is your married name? Your husband's last name?"

Elsie flinched so slightly at the mention of her husband, Alexis might have missed it if she hadn't been looking for changes that signaled Elsie's softening. Instead, the opposite occurred. Her face tightened again. "It was his last name, yes."

"How long have you been a widow?" Gabe didn't look up from the camera lens that held his attention.

Alexis's flinch could have beaten Elsie's in a contest, both in depth and endurance. *Gabe, oh wise one, she didn't say he died. They might have divorced. You don't know.*

"Ten years. And I'm not 'a widow.' I'm widowed. I'm a *woman* who has been widowed." Elsie waited.

Gabe stopped fiddling with the lens. "My mistake," he said. "I apologize."

Relationship crisis over, as far as Gabe was concerned, it appeared. How did he do that? Step in goo, and then bounce back to normal seconds later? The epitome of a sanguine personality. Alexis still felt the sting of Elsie's "widow" label, and she hadn't been the one to say it. Could she and Gabe *be* any more different?

"So, we were talking about your heritage," Alexis said. "Maternal? Paternal?"

Elsie waved her off. "Mutts. All of us. Won't help you."

"You mentioned your father is partial to cherry strudel. Does he have a German background?"

Elsie tipped her chin, her face as thickly fogged as the air over the lake earlier in the morning. She stood and turned toward the sink. She swiped a dishcloth over a counter that hadn't looked dirty. "No."

Alexis looked to Gabe for support. He stared back and shrugged his shoulders. The skin at her temples stretched tight. The thin muscles underneath throbbed. It would be so easy to walk away. The Heart-and-Home *Restoring Christmas* challenge already leaned heavily on the challenge side—no prior contact with the home owner, limited budget, strict time frame, real-time Christmas gathering at the conclusion. And now, a home owner who seemed to have no interest in changing anything, little imagination, and no desire to talk about either.

Giving back the money wouldn't be a problem. Giving up the possibility of a career-altering boost with national television coverage was no small thing. But holding on to her sanity was no small thing, either. Aunt Sarah would tell her to trust the Trustworthy One, to hand the decision making over to the God who knew more than she did and who—she could hear Sarah's counsel—"knows the end from the beginning."

Alexis bowed her head. It seemed appropriate for a moment like this. Instead of something holy-sounding, all she could think to pray was, *"Do You have this? Because I sure don't."*

"Do what you want." Elsie hadn't turned, but spoke toward the peeling wallpaper backsplash behind the sink.

"What do you mean?" Alexis felt for her pen and notepad on the tabletop. It might actually be time to record ideas.

"I mean what I said." Elsie faced them. "Do whatever it is you want to do. On the inside. But I have my reasons for wanting things a certain way on the outside. Understood?"

Trust the Trustworthy One. What do you know? Though she forced her face to behave itself, Alexis's heart danced. Full-steam ahead. She tossed a quick "*Thanks*" heavenward.

"Well," Gabe said as they left Elsie in the kitchen and headed through the back entrance to greet the arriving construction team, "it looks as if God has a vested interest in your being involved in *Restoring Christmas*, if you know what I mean."

It wasn't until she stood in the middle of the driveway, surrounded by falling leaves and a scattering of chickens, that she figured out what he meant. Both the thought and the fact that Gabe seemed at ease mentioning God's name made up for the fact she'd forgotten to grab her coat.

CHAPTER SEVEN

PREP FOR DEMO TOOK LONGER than the entire demolition process. Confining the majority of the labor to the first floor meant hauling some of the furniture and Elsie's personal items—pictures, lamps, kitchenware—to a spare room on the second floor. The rest made its way to a barn-like outbuilding that would serve as a temporary storage unit. Another outbuilding, no doubt once the home of equipment that farmed the hilly, rocky land, was set up as a makeshift workshop.

"Goats? She has goats, too?" Gabe backed out of a space between two buildings, camera rolling, followed by a stocky, short-legged animal bleating its territorial rights.

Alexis set the kitchen chair she carried at the entrance of the storage building and snapped a picture of the Gabe Goat Chase with her phone. It wouldn't make the *Restoring Christmas* video package, but she couldn't leave it out of her project journal.

Because Elsie insisted on living at the house during the construction phase, the team taped heavy plastic draping over doorways, windows, and heat vents. She insisted a hot plate, a college dorm–sized refrigerator, and jugs of water hauled to her bedroom on the second floor would "do her just fine" for a pretend kitchen during that phase of the remodeling. Alexis had to give Elsie credit. Once she was on board, she committed to the inevitable inconveniences without complaint. Without an *excess* of complaints.

"Won't an indoor bathroom take too much space out of my back hallway?"

"Not only will it be worth it," Alexis assured her, "but the redesign is going to make your hallway and kitchen feel even more spacious in spite of our stealing a few square feet for your bathroom. You'll see."

"Rather have a larger chicken coop."

Alexis sighed. "You're really fond of those birds, aren't you, Elsie?"

"Oh, goodness, no. They drive me crazy. But I am fond of fresh eggs. And having some to give away."

By the day's end, the home had been emptied, all the plastic dust barriers hung, and the task timeline board adjusted in conference with Ralph Abel and his Abel-Bodied Construction team. Given the PR opportunity for the business and the few weeks to the firm deadline, Ralph and his employees had agreed to work Saturday without the addition of overtime so they could get the unwanted walls removed, an I-beam installed for additional support, and— if all went well—the bathroom framed in and ready for the plumber.

"Ready to call it a day?" Gabe put the lens cap on his shoulder-saddle camera and slid it into its resting place in the back of his van.

"More than ready. That was intense." Alexis stretched her back muscles. She reached her arms overhead then moved them in a circle one at a time.

"You do that like an ex–ballet dancer."

"Ex–? I could still do ballet . . . if I wanted to."

"Ooh. *Hostile* ex–ballet dancer."

Alexis shoved her purse and laptop case onto the floor of the passenger side of the van. "I gave up ballet when—" *He does not need to know your entire life history.*

Gabe offered his arm for her to lean on as she climbed into the van. She used the armrest and the back of the seat instead. "Gave up ballet when . . . ?"

This was the man she needed to capture the best sides of her on film. The man she depended on to soften the angles and make sure shadows didn't turn her professional designer image into Goth at its worst—Halloween-like—for the video. If he was a childhood friend, rather than a new acquaintance, Aunt Sarah would have told her to "make nice."

"The family couldn't afford it. Something had to go." *Ballet lessons. And me.*

"Hey, I'm sorry about that. Someday, huh?"

"Someday what?" She pulled the seat belt across her coat-fattened torso.

"You'll get back to it. Right?"

"I passed that window of opportunity a few years ago. What ballet company would take on a—?"

"Doesn't have to be professionally. I just meant, if it gave you joy, don't give it up forever. Just for you." He turned the key in the ignition. "I'm still dealing with the aftereffects of killer chili. Can't eat that again until my stomach lining returns to normal. Want to stop for a fish dinner on our way home?"

She'd had smoother invitations to dinner before. She'd also had experience with guys like Gabe who assumed too much too fast. *Time to rein that in.* "You do realize we don't have to be . . . Let me rephrase that. We can't be together all the time."

"Oh. Right. You have so many *other* friends here in Algoma."

"Did you mean that to be as unkind as it sounded?"

Gabe navigated the narrow bridge across the sullen creek. "First, until this project is finished, we *do* have to be together practically all the time, so we're going to have to get used to it. Which is apparently harder for you than it is for me. Second, I can see why you thought that sounded snarky. Third, I regret that words and tone of voice can't be retracted. Fourth"—he braked extra long at the spot where the driveway met the side road—"it's good fish. Guaranteed."

"I'm choking on my own dust," she said, slapping at her pant leg to prove it. "I need to shower and change."

"Then we'll get it to-go. You can order by phone while I drive. It should be ready by the time we pull up to the restaurant. Then when we get home, you can go downstairs to eat your dinner. I'll stay out of your way upstairs. And I'll send the footage from today electronically. You can text me with the changes you want for tomorrow."

The van didn't move. She was going to have to say something. The plan sounded unnecessarily complicated, and it was her fault. "Okay." She dug out her phone. *And who's the boss here?* "Do you have the number memorized?"

His head-nod barely detectible, he said, "I do."

"Let's order a dinner for your dad, too. My treat."

Gabe's smile returned. "We'd both appreciate that. Thanks."

ALEXIS HIT REPLAY and watched the footage again. The man had an eye for capturing emotive moments. The art in a pile of weather-worn boards. A rusty hinge. A feather caught between floorboards of the porch. The movement of the late October wind against a fieldstone house that stood its ground.

What Gabe couldn't do, however, was grab any footage of Alexis when she wasn't at her worst. The short bits they'd shot as filler and introductions all showed her with a deep crease between her eyebrows or her hair sticking up on top like one sorry rabbit ear. She looked like a flustered, overheated amateur. *Good casting.*

She should have gone with her instincts and spent the money to get her hair done, colored, and cut into a more flattering style before making her way north. Tomorrow, she'd remove her coat, even for the outdoor scenes. And stand up straighter. And get her teeth whitened. She pressed two fingers against the crease between her eyebrows. What were the odds she'd find a Botox supplier in Algoma, Wisconsin? Duct tape was not the answer to everything.

The program producers wanted nitty-gritty? That was all she had to offer. They'd suggested rough camera work, a homegrown look. Even Gabe's attempts at homegrown came across as artistic.

And she'd mourned having to use a local videographer.

Her phone alerted her to a text message, from an unknown number. Ralph Abel? Who else could it be? She opened the text.

George Langley here. Thanks for the fish. I was feeling sorry for myself, losing out on the opportunity to work with a designer like you. Stuck here while you two young people are having all the fun. Can't even make myself a tuna sandwich without pain. And here comes Gabe with dinner, courtesy of you.

The text message spread out over three green clouds, but they kept coming.

Hope you liked Gabe's work. Don't tell him I said so, but he's miles ahead of where I was at his age. The boy has a gift. And you make beautiful subject matter for each frame.

The man was on high-powered pain medicine, obviously. Or the back injury had pinched off oxygen to his brain.

I've done a lot of video work over the years. Missing this opportunity is hard on me, I have to say. Love the concept of restoring Christmas. The symbolism of what you're doing is powerful. Not just for Elsie.

Did George know Elsie? He must. She'd lived in the community long enough to be part of its fabric. Small town. George probably knew everyone and vice versa. Maybe Alexis could gather intel about Elsie from Gabe's dad. If she didn't find a way to connect with her client . . .

Restoring Christmas.

It wasn't about her hair.

BEFORE SHE TURNED OUT the light, Alexis sent a text to Gabe.

Eating cold cereal for breakfast in the morning.

He immediately texted back.

Me, too, then. See you in the breezeway at seven-thirty. The crew arrives at eight. We don't want to miss the first swing of the sledgehammer.

GABE HAD THE VAN running when Alexis topped the stairs. He got out to offer an arm to lean on, as if he had no recollection of the previous evening. She slid her purse and laptop bag into the van and leaned on his arm for support as she climbed in.

"Heavy frost," she said.

"Look again. It snowed last night. We're supposed to get a couple of inches today."

She sank against the seat back. "Can't anything go right? I need a couple of warm days for painting the outside trim. We can't leave it as it is."

Gabe tapped a thermal cup in one of two holders between them. "This one's yours. Roasted Chestnut Latte. Extra whip."

She would have protested the extra whip, but it sounded somehow fortifying. "You ate cold cereal, then went to Tlazo to get this?"

"And this." He tapped his own cup. "Snow could be gone as early as tomorrow. We get lake-effect snow here, but we also get moderate temps, too, from being surrounded by water. Even though Door County technically starts a few miles north of here, we get to share some of its climate benefits."

"Is it too optimistic of me to expect a white Christmas this year?"

"It would sure help from the video perspective." Gabe flipped on the windshield wipers as new flakes fell.

"Farmers, videographers, and outdoor wedding planners."

"What?"

"They all long for perfect conditions. Rarely get them."

Gabe turned off the squealing wipers. The snow had stopped. "And moms-to-be ready to give birth to the Son of God." He glanced her way. "It fits. Perfect conditions would have been nice. But He came anyway."

Gabe's glass was so half-full. And he apparently saw Christmas in everything. Everything.

Alexis used the travel time—short as it was—to look over the plan for the day.

"Making a list?" Gabe asked. "Checking it twice?"

"The Christmas references will never end with you, will they?"

"Not until the project's over."

She looked at his profile behind the wheel. Sturdy but not intimidating. Did the corners of his mouth ever turn down? "Good."

"Good? I thought you'd branded me Mr. Irritation."

"When did I say that?" *Had she?* "Your Christmas references keep me on track. The calendar might say we're tiptoeing into November, but everything we're doing in the remodel and design is headed toward a singular destination—Christmas."

He tilted his head as if considering the validity of what she'd said. "Christmas is more of a launch pad than a destination, isn't it?"

Sometimes he could be so . . . irritating.

CHAPTER EIGHT

THE NOTE TACKED TO the back door hadn't weathered the snow, light as it was. The envelope opened with no resistance. The note inside unfolded more like fragile fabric than paper. Fabric with barely legible, smudged ink marks.

"What does it say?" Gabe asked, kicking the toes of his shoes alternately against the cement stoop.

Alexis squinted and read, "'Have to be gone a couple of days. You know where everything is. Or was. Elsie.'"

"I don't blame her for wanting to escape the mess we're making." Gabe shifted the weight of his shoulder bag of equipment.

"Why wouldn't she have said something yesterday? Or called me? She has my number."

"Bigger question, boss. How are we going to get in?"

It would have been foolish to leave a key in the envelope, but Alexis checked anyway. Nothing. She reached to run her hand above the door frame, but Gabe took over when it became clear she couldn't get close, even on tiptoe. She checked under the overturned bucket beside the door. At the base of what had months earlier housed a potted plant. Gabe lifted every rock large enough to hide a key.

One of Elsie's barn cats, one that had taken to Gabe the day before, wound its way between Alexis's feet as if drawing a figure eight with the tip of her tail. "Move, cat. We're on a mission." The animal jangled with each step.

"Who puts a bell on a barn cat?" Gabe asked. "Elsie, that's who." He squatted to cat level and scrubbed at the fur around her neck. "Eureka."

"I think Elsie called her Tabitha." Alexis took a step back.

"Eureka, I found it!" Gabe unclipped something on the cat's collar and held it aloft. The key.

"How did Elsie know Tabitha would come to us? We could have been locked out all day."

"I'm a cat whisperer."

"That's a scary thought."

Gabe slipped the key into the lock. "It gained us entrance, did it not?" He stood aside to let her through.

"But will it gain us entrance into the storage shed? The note also says she got a late delivery last night. I hope that means the things I ordered arrived." She pushed the plastic drape aside and walked into the kitchen. "Ooh. They're here."

Alexis bent to read the labels of several of the dozen boxes stacked in the middle of the kitchen floor. They'd all been opened. Probably Elsie. Each box was marked with a one-word notation in the same penmanship as the note in Alexis's hand.

"OK."

"OK."

"OK."

"No."

"No."

"No!"

The pattern continued. Not even one box held anything more positive than "OK." No "beautiful" or "gorgeous" or "stunning." And what was Alexis supposed to do with the items marked with an emphatic "No!"?

"Aw. The pressed-tin backsplash. She hates it. I thought she'd love it."

Gabe peered into the box. "Maybe she doesn't mind the idea of tin, but didn't like the palm frond design."

"They're not palm fronds. They're gingko leaves." *Obviously.*

"Uh-huh. They're . . . big." He drew one out of the box and held it against the kitchen wall at backsplash height. "Big. Are they also . . . returnable?"

Alexis sank to the floor beside the stack of boxes. She narrowed her eyes to slits. "I don't question your camera angles."

"Sure you do. And you should. You're the project manager. It's your career, ultimately."

"But you can question my design skills?" She crossed her arms, fully aware that her body language was speaking much more vociferously than her voice.

He sat on the floor, out of kicking range, she noticed.

"I'm not questioning your design skills or tastes at all, Alexis. I've seen your work."

He had? "Where?"

"Nice website, by the way. If I was going to question anything, it would be . . . "

"What? What would you question?" *Do anger management classes help a person recognize when their hands are turning into fists? Do they offer an alternative more significant than counting to ten? Does anger management come in an online version? Aunt Sarah has been asking what I want for Christmas. I now have an idea.*

"It's the nature of the contest," Gabe said. "They don't give you the opportunity to get to know the client before you create the design plan, order style-specific items . . . "

"These were custom-made."

"Whoa. That's . . . that's intriguing. For a fieldstone farmhouse?"

Alexis uncrossed her arms and rubbed her palms on her knees. "I liked the juxtaposition of the very modern and the very ancient and the—"

"I don't think Elsie knows how to juxtapose."

Something—the quirk in his mouth, the softness in his eyes, the kindness in his voice—deflated her ballooning exasperation.

He slid closer to her. "It seems to me . . . Never mind."

"You've gone this far. Say it."

"Isn't listening a designer's greatest asset?"

What did he know about design? Alexis's exhale stirred dust that littered the sorry-looking linoleum floor. "Elsie won't tell me anything."

"We know a lot about her from what she's said . . . and what she hasn't said."

"Like, what?" Crossing her arms was a reflex, not a decision.

"She loves, admires, and is devoted to her father. She's distant from her children and their families, and not just in miles. She appreciates this place and isn't eager for it to feel other than what it is."

"You can say that again." *Isn't eager.* Understatement of the year.

"But I won't, because you know it. You listened to that much." Gabe drew a deep breath.

"Go on."

"She respects you, Alexis."

"Where did you get that idea?" And why did her name sound better coming out of Gabe's mouth than she'd heard before?

Gabe rested his elbow on the nearest cardboard box. "She let you move forward. She left you a key to carry on when she isn't here to supervise. She's going through with her end of the agreement."

Alexis had to find a new position. One leg had fallen asleep. The other was on its way.

"Elsie likes simple things with deep meaning," Gabe said.

"She didn't tell us that."

"She served cherry strudel, not because it's *her* favorite, but because it's her dad's."

The almost-November sun tiptoed across the floor. It warmed the circle in which they sat. If Kewaunee County, Door County, and Algoma perched between them followed Chicago's example, November would be marked by more gray days than sun-filled. She let herself savor every candlewatt of energy sending the dust motes flying. "She likes eggs more than she likes raising chickens," Alexis said, experimenting with the analysis Gabe apparently found natural.

"Correct."

"And owning a showcase house isn't on her agenda." As soon as the words left her lips, a coil in her brain relaxed its tension.

"Also correct."

"She doesn't do anything for show. She's intentional. Elsie isn't afraid of hard work." Alexis paused. "She appreciates bold color."

Gabe's brows furrowed. "She does?"

"The tomato-red teapot?"

"So, she's comfortable with *small* touches of bold color."

Alexis mentally toured what she remembered about Elsie's house before it had been emptied. Had the woman furnished her home with whatever she could find in secondhand stores? Or had those furnishings lived with her for decades, when she was still married? What were her favorite colors? All of them? What lay at the heart of her personality . . . when not under the stress Alexis had caused her?

"Gabe, you have to know this isn't how I normally handle my clients. They talk. I listen. I create a design plan that fits their tastes and personalities, even when I ask them to trust me with an element that stretches them a little." Or, that was her intention, anyway.

"I believe you."

"This challenge is different in so many ways. So far beyond how I imagined it would test me." Her laughter sounded nerve-based, even to her own ears. "And we've barely started."

"Drink your coffee."

"Excuse me?"

"You'll need it. I believe that's the Abel-Bodied work crew heading up the driveway."

Seven and a half weeks before she could breathe again.

"And Alexis?"

"Yes?"

"Can I be bold and say one more thing?"

Bolder than you already are, Camera Guy? "Sure."

"Elsie made me think of it. Ask yourself if your assignment is to *reinvent* Christmas or *restore* it."

ELSIE HAD PICKED the noisiest day of the project to be gone. Maybe she saw it coming and decided to visit her estranged grandkids or something. Alexis didn't know, and resisted calling Elsie's cell phone for fear the woman would ask what the designer had decided to do with her fieldstone home.

For now, the answer would have to remain, "I don't know. I only know the next step. One step. The next one."

Gabe Langley would probably tie that to Christmas somehow.

"Joseph, what are you doing traveling when Mary's so close to her due date?"

"It's a decree. We have to be counted for the tax census in Bethlehem. So, we're headed to Bethlehem."

"What are you going to do after you get there, if the baby should come?"

"I don't know. I only know the next step. One step. We're going to Bethlehem."

Gabe Langley. If he wasn't so annoying, she might let herself consider . . .

No. That could only end badly. Either she would mess it up or he would. Story of her life where men were concerned. Plus, she needed focus, not another distraction.

Speaking of the younger Mr. Langley, where was he?

A *thud* rattled the windows and sent a chunk of plaster from the ceiling to the white plastic lid of Alexis's coffee cup. She threw her body across her laptop—which was perched on a box in the middle of the kitchen—and waited for another *thud*. Instead, she heard what sounded like a touchdown celebration in the living room.

"What's going on here, guys?" *Hands on hips too much? Probably.* She put them instead in the small of her back and stretched out the kinks she'd acquired from the awkward angle when using a stack of boxes as a makeshift desk.

"Whoa. You should have been here for that," one of Ralph's workers said. "Our man Gabe is 'strong like ox.'" The worker's affected Eastern European accent capped the comment.

Another round of whoops circled the room. The objects of their attention were her landlord, leaning on the handle of a sledgehammer, and a three-foot-across gaping hole in the wall just behind him.

"One blow," Ralph Abel said, shaking his head. "You gonna be around for the rest of this project, Gabe?"

"He is," Alexis said. *"Behind* . . . the . . . camera."*

"I'm on a federal- and state-mandated ten-minute break," he said, stirring affirmation from the others bedecked in tool belts. "Although"—he rotated his camera shoulder—"that's probably my last feat of strength for a while, men. I don't get paid the big bucks like you do." He tossed the sledgehammer to one of the construction workers and reached for his travel mug. "Oh!" He grabbed his shoulder.

"Gabe?" In her mind, Alexis wrestled with getting closer to see whether he was okay or getting closer so she could slug him in the other arm.

"Kidding. Acting!" He raised his sledgehammer arm above his head and bowed to the applause.

"May I remind you gentlemen that we have a very tight

schedule to keep? The plumber will be here Monday at oh-dark-thirty. Will we be ready?"

"Getting back to work, ma'am. Yes, ma'am. Right away, boss."

A chorus of faux kowtowing brought her to the edge of apologizing for her tone. She resisted. "And by the way, men, breaks are a recommendation. Not a mandate."

"Careful," Gabe whispered as he passed her. "They'll think you've quit caffeine cold turkey."

"Huh?"

"Do you know the difference between *boss* and *bossy*, Alexis? One letter. *Y*. Get it? *Why?*" He peeled back a chunk of the drywall he'd dislodged. "Hey."

"You couldn't possibly have known what I was thinking."

"Alexis. Come look at this."

"At what? Oh." She stopped, her hands clasped under her chin. "That's . . . amazing. Is it all through this wall?"

"Looks like it."

Her pulse quickened.

Gabe's expression looked like a little boy who'd just found where his mom hid the Christmas presents. "Are you thinking what I'm thinking?"

"Reclaimed wood?"

"Reclaimed wood," he said.

"And an heirloom tomato-red couch."

Gabe frowned. "Christmas red."

She smiled. "Whatever."

CHAPTER NINE

ALEXIS'S FIFTY-DEGREE WEATHER came six days into November. Jacket temps turned into sweatshirt temps. As the crew shifted work to the exterior, shirtsleeves replaced sweatshirts and flannel.

None of her design projects had been filmed before. Nothing more than the video she captured on her camera to document befores-and-afters, or sweeping views for her website. She hadn't needed to be in front of the camera for those. Picking her wardrobe for each day added to the list of tricky maneuvers for the *Restoring Christmas* project.

In a one-hour program, viewers would see progress emerge over the course of the two months of filming. She couldn't wear one of the same two or three outfits for every scene. Some days were heavy-lifting days, or paint days, like this one. Others were planned shots, where she described a technique or finish.

Gabe's dad had overheard her clothing moan and volunteered a solution. Gabe's mom's clothes had been sitting idle in storage bins in the garage since her death. George's intention had always been to give them to charity. He didn't know why he'd hesitated passing them on to someone else for almost a year. He had other reminders of how much she'd meant to them both.

She hadn't worn them *while* she died, Alexis reminded herself. It wasn't creepy. It was a sweet gesture on George's part—a way for him to see something of his wife's embedded in the project his son created. A sweet gesture.

"You might not find anything you like," Gabe had said. "But Mom was a class act in every way. I'll go get the bins."

Alexis found plenty of shirts, blouses, sweaters, and jewelry to boost her on-camera wardrobe. Mrs. Langley had good taste. Alexis wished she'd had a chance to know her.

When she showed up for breakfast the first time she wore something of Gabe's mom's, Gabe made no comment. Which would be more awkward? Talking about it or ignoring the issue? Alexis plunged in. "This is your mom's shirt."

"I know."

"I love the color." She stroked the fabric on the sleeve.

"It looks good on you."

"Are you going to be okay with this reminder of your grief?"

Gabe had squinted as if he hadn't understood the question. "I look at it as a reminder of how vibrant she was, not how much I miss her."

"Good. You'd tell me if it started to bother you, though, right?"

He didn't answer for several moments. "Mom always wore that with a blue-jean vest."

"Then I never will. Reminders and grief walk the same fence line."

Gabe seemed lost in thought. "You know a few things about grief, don't you, Alexis? Who did you lose that you loved?"

Other than my tenacious Aunt Sarah? Just about everybody.

"I LIKE THAT ONE on you, too," Gabe said as Alexis brushed bits of construction debris from the shoulders of a plum fine-gauge sweater a few days later.

She stepped around a yet-to-be-repaired floorboard on the porch. "This is my own."

"I know." Gabe ducked behind the tripod camera and said, "It . . . it frames well."

Ah. Always in videographer mode. "Elsie said she'd be out in a minute with a new idea for the trim color. We should probably get some footage of our discussing that."

"Ready to go. The lighting is great right now."

"Where do you want us to stand?"

"Let's put Elsie in the porch chair and you there, but sitting on the porch, legs dangling over the edge. That way you'll be looking up at her as you talk."

His area of expertise. He did have a gift. "Like this?"

He made an adjustment on the camera. "Nice."

Elsie came around the corner of the house carrying her egg basket. "I think I found a sample of the color I want for the trim and shutters," she said.

Please, Lord. Tell me she's given up on the idea of beige-bland. "That dark straw color of your basket won't provide much contrast against the fieldstone, Elsie."

Gabe kept his distance but slipped behind Elsie. The cameras were rolling.

"Not the basket," the older woman said. "What's in it." She withdrew a couple of pale turquoise eggs and handed one to Alexis.

"Turquoise? *Faded* turquoise?"

"In egg breeder terms, it's blue. From my Araucanas. The rumpless chickens with the funny moustache tufts."

The egg was still warm. Alexis worked hard to avoid looking directly at the cameraman. From the corner of her eye, she saw him holding back a comment.

"The color would be beautiful against the stone, Elsie, but unusual for—"

"Has to be this color."

Alexis told her objections to wait in line. Time to listen. "It has to be?"

"Yes." When she pursed her lips like that, tiny lines appeared to splay out like a child would draw sunbeams flung from a bright yellow circle in a blue-crayoned sky. "I have my reasons."

Alexis calculated how much of her exterior Christmas decorations she'd have to adjust for the new color scheme. She could keep the coppery red berries and the greenery. New ribbon for the wreath she'd imagined for the front door. *Oh, the door.* "Elsie, your front door has seen better days."

"Like most of us."

"And it isn't really in keeping with the style of the home." Alexis opened her ever-present laptop and awakened the screen. "What do you think of this option?"

Sunburst again.

"Or, this one?"

"They have windows in them."

Here we go. "They'll let in a little more light, but these two models have internal shades, so with just a flip of a switch, you can block the light or add privacy, if you want. This model even comes with a remote, so you can close the shade from the comfort of your couch or favorite chair." Hope could sound artificial if she wasn't careful.

"No window in the door."

"If you're worried about safety . . . "

"That's not it."

Gabe moonwalked to catch another angle.

Eyes on your client, Alexis. Eyes on your client. "You have no room for a sidelight door assembly, where you can catch light and see who might be at the door before opening it. I'd hate to have us try to bust through the stone. And a new, wider header would cost . . . "

Elsie removed the egg from Alexis's hand. The chicken expert probably noticed how Alexis's eagerness to convince her client had translated into egg-worrying. "I have a picture in my mind. The front door has boards running vertically. Same dusty Araucanas egg color as the trim. A black iron latch. Can you do that?"

Gabe's artistic sense and his skill at catching "a moment" likely had him zooming in on her for her response. Alexis let the tension out of her facial muscles and answered, "Sure, we can, Elsie. I think that will look beautiful." *Especially nice when the copper roof is new. Stunning, in fact.*

The home owner waited for Gabe's Hollywoodish "That's a wrap!" before leaving the porch with her basket of eggs. When she was out of range, Gabe said, "Pick your battles?"

"Exactly."

"Nice comeback, boss." Gabe capped the camera lens.

"What?"

"*Eggs*-actly?"

"Think Christmas, Gabe. Not Easter."

Gabe shouldered one camera and picked up the tripod. "You can't have one without the other."

"Ooh, deep," she said, just a smidge of mocking in her voice.

"Ooh, truth," he said in return. "Want me to run for the paint?"

"Would you? I have to search online for an unconventional door with next-day delivery."

"Be back in a few. Oh."

Alexis logged on to her favorite architectural supply distributor website. "What?"

"I can't leave without the egg," Gabe said. "Now that we've found the perfect shade."

By the time Gabe returned, the air had warmed another few degrees, Alexis had placed her door order, cringing at the cost of next-day delivery, and the plumbing inspector had come and gone, giving his blessing on the crew's efforts.

Alexis changed clothes and grabbed a paintbrush. The sun hadn't slowed its path across the sky. The trim paint needed every advantage it could get. Gabe shot a few frames, then set his camera aside and picked up a paintbrush.

One of the Abel-Bodied construction workers opted for extension ladder duty and the second floor trim.

"On a day like this, it's hard to believe we could be standing knee-deep in snow a week from now." Gabe followed the edge of the door frame with his angled brush.

"Is that from the forecast or your imagination?" She finished her first window and stood back to check the effect.

"I haven't looked at the forecast for next week. But it could happen."

"I've lived through a handful of Chicago winters. Not much about winter catches me by surprise anymore." She stepped off the porch and walked to a spot mid-yard, then turned back to get the full view. Nice. Very nice, in fact. A softer image than the bold Madagascan brown she'd planned. But she liked it.

Gabe joined her in the yard. "Looks good so far. I take it you're pleased?"

"Definitely makes a statement. I don't know what that statement is, but . . . "

"I bought a couple of quarts for the door in a shade a tick darker than the trim. How would you feel about that?" He looked at her with a comical expression that didn't need words to say, "Did I do good, boss?"

Do you have flaws, Gabe Langley? Other than overexuberance and an excess of optimism? You must. We all do. What are they? Should I be wary of what I don't yet know about you? "I almost called you when you were at the paint store to suggest that very thing," she said.

"Did not."

"Did too."

"What stopped you?"

"Insecurity, I suppose." The words were out of her mouth before she could consider the danger of her cameraman, landlord, and . . . friend-in-the-making . . . knowing that potentially damaging bit of information. Too late now.

Gabe scraped specks from his paintbrush handle with his thumbnail. "Dad thinks he might be able to go to church on Sunday."

I don't mind changing the subject. "That's good. I'm glad his pain is easing."

"The only thing is . . . "

"What is it?"

"I'm in the sound booth on Sunday, so that means two services in a row, plus the time between. That's too much for him to endure, until he's back to normal. He'll be doing well to sit through one service."

"Yes," she sighed with appropriate melodrama. "I will haul your dad to church on Sunday."

"I'm sure he'll appreciate the 'haul' reference."

Alexis picked at dots of paint on her own brush handle. "You know what I meant."

"If you bring him to the second service, we can drop him off at home and then go to the Flying Pig afterward."

"When pigs fly."

"You don't have to be rude." Gabe turned his petulant child expression on her, especially ridiculous on a man with his height and athletic build.

"I assume that's where the restaurant derived its name," she said. "From the 'when pigs fly' adage."

Gabe started toward the porch with Alexis at his heels. "It's not a restaurant. It's a gift shop, gallery, garden sort of thing. Sunday is their last farmer's market of the season. I have an idea for music for the Christmas dinner scenes."

"Every time you start with 'I have an idea,' I get this funny feeling in my stomach." She dipped her paintbrush into the soft turquoise paint and let the excess drip off the tip.

"That feeling," Gabe said, reaching for the bare trim where the stone exterior met the porch ceiling, "is called joy."

"No. I'm pretty sure it's indigestion."

"But you'll come to church with us on Sunday?"

"I have to, don't I? I'm your dad's chauffeur." And she owed both of them for providing a place for her to "kick back."

CHAPTER TEN

IT WASN'T THAT ALEXIS hadn't attended church before. She was, as they say, a regular. In childhood, she'd appreciated the sense of belonging and safety, and soaked up stories of Bible characters who were brave in the face of adversity and who saw impossible things happen in their lives when God showed up.

In her teen years, she'd attended church because Aunt Sarah said it was "good for her." And she owed it to her aunt.

College meant the choice was hers alone. She chose sleep more often than not. Until her senior year, when she let herself get drawn into a volunteer project with Habitat for Humanity and made friends with a circle of people from a community church not far from campus. The childhood sense of belonging and safety returned, as did her fascination with God-given courage.

Because she got a job in the area, going to church fell into the category of routine, although she'd steadfastly resisted getting too involved beyond Sunday morning. She had her career to think about. Beyond college age, but not yet part of the couples or couples-with-babies scene, she contented herself with a nod to God on Sunday mornings and the assumption that He hovered somewhere nearby if she needed Him.

So, George and Gabe's Seaside Fellowship shouldn't have been that much of a shock to her system.

She and George had settled in the back row on the right-side aisle, in case he needed to get up and walk around to keep his back from "seizing up," as he put it. Gabe waved at them from the sound booth just behind them to the left.

Most of the people in the almost-full sanctuary stood when they sang the opening worship songs. Alexis did whatever George did. Sat when he sat. Stood when he stood, in case he needed an arm to lean on.

The songs were familiar enough that she could sing along, with a couple of newer songs she hadn't heard. She followed the lyrics on the screens on either side of the worship team. Concepts she knew, but worded in a way that breathed new life into them. Something in the look of one of the guitar players as he worshiped told her he may have taken the hard route to get to this place. Playing guitar for worship might not have been where he'd started. The light in his eyes and gratitude that expressed itself in his body language stirred her. She'd seen it among some of her college friends.

And Gabe. She'd seen it in Gabe, come to think of it.

When the music segued into the sermon, Alexis pulled out a pen and small notepad. While the pastor droned about things she already knew, she could make notes about the week's work schedule and sketch ideas for how she'd eventually turn Elsie's reimagined first floor into a holiday showpiece.

But the pastor didn't drone. And the notes she took related to sagging faith, not sagging floor joists. She'd filled three pages with thoughts to consider later when the pastor said, "Let's pray."

What? She checked her phone for the time. He'd been speaking for forty minutes and it had felt like ten.

George tapped her arm and whispered, "I think I'd better leave before I get crushed by the crowd. They're a hugging bunch. Not sure my back can take that today."

She grabbed her things and followed him out while the pastor prayed with words as heartfelt, genuine, and practical as she'd remembered hearing.

"Can't thank you enough for this," George said when they reached the parking lot. "Good for my soul." His steps ginger and slow, he headed in the direction of her car.

"Let me drive up for you. Stay right here." She took off before he could object. *I missed having the chance to do this for my parents. Not that I wanted them to be needy.* She reached the car and slid behind the drivers' seat. *Not needy. But maybe to be around to need me.*

The lake wore blue today to complement the unusually deep blue sky that arched over it. When she turned the car onto the highway to head north, back into Algoma, George asked if she minded if he rolled down the window.

"It's too cold for that," he said, "but I could use a good dose of fresh air."

"Go right ahead." She couldn't imagine how bored he must be, stuck inside while his back healed in baby steps, with him unable to drive. He'd mentioned more than once how grieved he was not to be the one serving as videographer for her project. What if Gabe was out of the picture and George had been the person she worked with day to day? Life might be simpler. Not necessarily better.

And with that thought, she determined to get her mind back in the game and out of fantasyland.

SHE MADE GEORGE a grilled ham and cheese sandwich for lunch and cut up fresh veggies to accompany it. He asked to see some of her revised plans for Elsie's house and commented on a point here and there.

He'd graduated to a recliner for naps and headed that way while Alexis put his dishes in the dishwasher.

"You don't have to do that. I'm not completely helpless," George said.

"You and Elsie would make a good pair." She chuckled. Then her stomach tightened and snuffed the laughter as quickly as a stiff wind would snuff an unprotected candle. Pair. The man lost his wife. Almost a year ago. "I mean, you're both fiercely determined."

"By that definition"—Gabe said, closing the breezeway

door behind him as he entered the room—"you and *I* would make a great pair."

"No argument there," George said, pulling his fleece blanket closer to his chest.

The wall clock ticked its presence too long in the silence.

"Well," George said, closing his eyes, "I imagine you two are as eager for the Flying Pig as I am for this nap that's coming on fast."

"Never been more eager to see a Flying Pig than I am today," Alexis said, snatching her coat from the back of a chair.

"Sorry it took me so long after church," Gabe said. "They're a bunch of huggers."

"So your dad led me to believe." She slid her purse handle over her shoulder.

"We didn't mind," George said. "Alexis is good company."

"I know, Dad. I know."

Definitely time to establish some workplace boundaries.

THE PARKING LOT at the Flying Pig, a little farther south than the church on the road that led to Alaska—the small Wisconsin village rather than the state of the same name—then Kewaunee along the lake, offered them two options for parking spaces. All the rest were filled.

"I wish you could see the gardens in the spring or summer, even earlier in the fall," Gabe said. "I do several weddings out here every year. I'll have to show you a few of the still shots sometime. If you're interested. But first, the farmer's market."

A section of the parking lot's southern driveway had been cordoned off for white roof-only or roof-and-back-only tent booths—a dozen or more. "Taste this," Gabe said, presenting her with a small plastic spoon dripping with local honey. "Basswood."

She took the spoon and leaned forward to keep the sticky substance from landing somewhere other than in her mouth. "Hmm. Good. I thought honey was honey."

The woman sitting at the table with jars of honey spread in front of her looked like she'd swallowed a bee.

Gabe took Alexis's arm and steered her toward the next booth while telling the woman, "You'll have to forgive her. She's from Chicago. She doesn't know any better."

"Gabe!"

The woman's laughter followed them to the next booth, with artisanal breads and multicolored root vegetables. Another booth offered samples of apples chilled naturally by the air. Varieties with which Alexis was well familiar—her Chicago roots notwithstanding—and others that were new to her.

"Let's get some fresh apple cider for the work crew," she said, reaching first for a half gallon, then changing her mind and choosing the gallon jug instead.

"Good idea," Gabe said, "but unless you want to carry that for the next half hour, I recommend we leave it here until we're done walking the whole route."

She paid for the cider at Gabe's suggestion, agreeing that with the size of the crowd, the booth might be sold out before they returned. The vendor marked her name on the plastic jug and set it on a back table.

"Homemade caramel corn?"

"It's addicting," Gabe said. "Keep walking. Here's what I wanted you to see." He took a rabbit trail from the path they'd been on and crossed to a booth with two young women musicians. One played harp. The other played cello.

Alexis hadn't realized the music was live until they neared the booth. Intoxicatingly mellow, the music they made set a perfect stage for the artsy, organic event. The gardens behind them, the bridge, gazebo, and metal sculptures all contributed to the sweetness of the scene. Soap bubbles floated past. Soap bubbles? One popped close to Alexis's nose. With Gabe's help.

"I'll show you the birdbath bubbles in a few minutes," Gabe said. "But listen to this music." He turned so his back faced the young musicians. "Don't you think it would be perfect for the Christmas dinner scene? Well, Christmas music, I mean. They can do Christmas music."

"They're very good. Let me guess. They've played for weddings where you were the videographer?"

"A few. I think we could set them up next to the fireplace, or opposite the . . . uh . . . copper tree . . . "

"Rethinking that. I might go with a cedar tree, from Elsie's property, with copper ornaments."

"I like it. There are a couple of Christmas village stores

in Door County. If you want to buy local, we could check those out."

We. He kept using the word *we.* It probably wasn't a bad thing that he saw the *Restoring Christmas* project as partly his. He was invested. An invested employee could be counted on to give his or her best effort.

Alexis took one of the business cards propped in the open cello case. "I'll call you," she said to the cellist as the music played on.

Hydroponic herbs, home-processed canned goods, fudge, cherry turnovers, cherry pies, tart cherry juice, Montmorency frozen cherries by the gallon, artwork, woven scarves, high-quality handmade pasta . . . Every booth provided either an education or something to satisfy the taste buds or the soul. A nice break from breathing construction dust and re-crunching numbers in the budget.

A Flying Pig statue perched high on the grain silo–shaped main building of the property. It looked on as they finished their trek through the farmer's market area and walked the gardens. Mostly dormant at this time of year, frost-nipped, or evergreen but stiffened by the cold that seeped through Alexis's coat, the gardens still held enchantment. Artistically, the evergreens rivaled the metal sculptures and glass elements positioned throughout. A small pond sported a growing edge of ice and a shed painted in wild colors stood at its far end.

"Getting cold?" Gabe asked as they circled back toward the main building.

"Reached that point long ago," she said.

"One more stop before we go inside and warm up." He led her to a giant birdbath with a plastic-handled hoop resting inside. He dipped the hoop in the birdbath's liquid contents and swept it through the chilled air. "I'm glad the wind died down," he said as massive, iridescent bubbles broke away from the hoop and floated around them. "You'd think this feature was for the kids, but you'll see more adults here than children. Try it."

She took the handle from him, redipped, then swiped. A bubble tried to form, but popped before it had a chance.

"Slower," he said. "Give the moment time to form. Use your ballerina arms." He swept his arms in wide, decidedly feminine circles.

"Gabe? People are watching."

He stopped, then lifted his palms upward. "And thank You, God, for this glorious day! Amen." He lowered his arms. "Do you want to go inside?"

"I certainly do."

The gift shop inside the Flying Pig looked as if it was between seasons, packing away the remnants of fall and unpacking for Christmas. Gabe excused himself while she meandered through the windowed room with unique gift items—jewelry, pottery, books, cards—curated by a manager with an obvious taste for quality. On a few items that caught her interest, she ventured to check the price tag. If she won the spot on the *Restoring Christmas* special, she could easily afford it. If she failed, she couldn't afford the tag the price was printed on.

"Favorite item?" Gabe asked, handing her a saucer-sized peanut butter cookie wrapped in cellophane.

"So many. Lots to admire. But, cookies before lunch?"

"Not to worry. They're gluten-free. No calories."

"That's not what gluten-free means."

"I know. Humor me. So, your favorite thing?"

She walked to a center display. "These earrings. That mug. This sign. This whole shelf of stoneware. Oh. Oh, Gabe."

"What?"

"Wouldn't Elsie love this set of turned candlesticks on her mantel?"

Gabe lifted one as if testing its heft. "You mean, the mantel she doesn't have yet?"

"Yeah, that one."

"They'd be great."

Alexis closed her eyes, imagining them against the backdrop of the reclaimed wood. "I think they'd be perfect . . . if they were marked at half price."

"I can make some like that."

"Gabe . . ."

"I know where I can find some salvaged newel posts and balusters. My friend has a wood lathe."

"Gabe . . ."

"You're supposed to say, 'You'd be willing to do that for the project? Oh, thank you so much, kind sir, because I completely trust you to do a magnificent job and I know they'll probably turn out even better than these which I can't possibly afford.'"

"You're cute when you're annoying."

"What was that first part?"

CHAPTER ELEVEN

"THIS HEARTH HASN'T BEEN warm in a long time."

Elsie, newly returned from another mystery trip, rubbed her hand along the fieldstone hearth near where she sat on its unforgiving surface.

"The crew thinks we can get the fireplace working again, Elsie." Alexis watched Elsie hold her hand to the draft of air slipping through the aged glass doors. "Or . . . we could install a gas insert or electric insert."

"Might as well watch the pilot light on my stove, for all the fun that would be."

Alexis pictured Elsie crouching to get a glimpse of her ancient stove's pilot light, while sipping hot chocolate. "A real fire is always the best, in my book."

"Mine, too."

"But it can be messy. And it takes a lot of energy to cut and split wood, or a lot of money to purchase it cut-and-split already. Plus carrying it in. Cleaning out the ashes."

"Sold. Real wood it is." She dusted her hands and stood, all seventy-two years of her.

"Elsie, are you sure? That's a lot of work."

"I'm not afraid of hard work. If I take after my dad's side of the family, which I suspect I do, I'll have twenty years—give or take—to enjoy a real fire again. And a warm hearth. Is that all you wanted out of me? I have things to do."

Alexis looked at the shell of a room in which they sat, open now to the kitchen area, but still a long way from habitable. "Yes, so do we." She started toward the kitchen. "I don't know if you noticed, but we found a shutter for the window that was missing one. It was in the tool shed. We scraped off the old paint and it is now a beautiful Araucanas blue like the others. Ralph is out there installing it now."

Elsie blanched. "No! Tell him to take it down! Never mind. I'll tell him." She marched toward the front door.

"What's wrong?"

"I don't want it replaced. That's what."

"Elsie, I don't understand." She followed the woman onto the porch, mid-November's biting wind stealing her breath and any semblance of thunder.

"Young man!" Elsie stood a few feet from the ladder anchored in snow and hollered up at the "young" fifty-year-old construction worker. "Stop it. Please. Stop with the shutter. I don't want it."

"Huh?" Ralph held the still-unattached shutter with one hand and a power drill with the other.

Alexis focused on keeping her voice even. "Elsie, I'm all for asymmetry when it fits the project. But this house really needs matching shutters on the windows. In the era and style this house was constructed—"

"No second shutter on that window. You said I could have my say with the exterior of the house."

The sting of the wind had nothing over the cutting edge of Elsie's words. The shiver that raced through Alexis had two roots. "Elsie, don't cry. Please don't cry. I don't understand it. But if it means that much to you, we'll work something out. Maybe we could install the shutter to film the exterior shots, then take it down after Christmas, when we pack up and leave. Would that work?"

"No. I don't know." Her cheeks reddened. "I'm a foolish old woman. I don't know what I'm saying. Or why. Maybe—"

Alexis wrapped her arm around the bent woman.

"Maybe I'll go the way of my father. Memories erased. Stolen by the disease. Maybe I'm already on that path."

Alexis steered Elsie toward the relative warmth of the empty, in-progress house. "Elsie, where do you go when you take off for days?"

"I'm not wandering, if that's what you think." Three fewer decibels and her response would have been indiscernible to the human ear.

"Are you trying to escape us?" Alexis asked. "This chaotic mess? Me? I would never want to cause you—"

"Where I go is my own business." Elsie stopped just inside the threshold and faced her. "But it doesn't have anything to do with you. I'm sorry if I made you feel that way. And the door"—she flattened her seven-decades-old hand against the surface of the door the color of a fancy chicken egg—"is . . . perfect." More tears.

Alexis was missing something important. What and where she'd find it remained a mystery.

"Going upstairs for a nap. Do you think you can get those men to hold down the noise?"

Was she serious?

Elsie patted her arm. Calmer now. "That's okay, honey. I once slept through a rocket launch at Cape Canaveral. You're . . . you're doing a good job."

"I hope we can get the bathroom finished up today. Then, maybe later we can talk about what would mean the most to include for the Christmas dinner. Food. People. Decorations with a tie to your family. The kinds of things that make Christmas special for you."

Elsie paused with her foot on the first step to the second story. "It'd be easier to talk about plumbing."

Alexis watched the woman take the steps slowly, leaning on the handrails on either side. She'd never seen her use the handrails before.

GABE BOUNCED INTO the living room on surprisingly light feet for his size. "I got the most amazing angles on the guys all crammed into that tiny bathroom. Funniest thing I ever saw. We'll add some voice-overs of you talking to the audience through the process. But you are going to love those scenes."

"That's . . . wonderful."

"What's wrong?"

Who else would she talk to about this? Who else would care? "Do you have time for a board meeting?"

"You mean . . . ?"

Alexis listened for the telltale creaking overhead as Elsie walked across the floor and the metallic sound of springs complaining as the woman lowered herself onto her iron bed. "A board meeting on the boardwalk."

"It'll be chillier than our Indian summer board meetings. That wind . . . "

"Maybe it'll help clear my head."

SNOW HAD STARTED to fall again by the time Gabe pulled the van into the parking lot by Crescent Beach. "Sure you want to go out there in this?" Gabe asked.

"You don't have to come, if you don't want to." Alexis pulled her hat over her ears and snugged her leather gloves. "But you were right. It's a good place to think. And that's what I need. With or without you."

"With."

Alexis exhaled the breath she'd been holding. "Fine, then. Let's go."

"Will I need my camera?"

"I need your brain and your heart for this one. Wait—let me rephrase that."

"No. That sounds good as it is." He leaned forward and shook his head, then slid two fingers onto his throat at about the spot where an EMT might check for a pulse. "Both seem to be in working order. We'd better get started before either takes a turn for the worse."

Her boots served her well as they navigated the accumulating snow to get to the boardwalk. "Are you always this blissfully carefree, Gabe? Gabe?"

He'd dropped a few paces behind her. She waited while he caught up. "I've known the flipside of carefree." He used his foot to scoot a drift of snow off the boardwalk into the pebbles and sand. "I like blissful better."

"Misspent youth?" *How far do I dare poke into his past?*

"Something like that. Misspent. Misused. Mistaken. Missed it."

She buttoned the coat she'd left open and doubled the scarf around her neck. "Missed what? What's the 'it,' if you don't mind my asking?" She drove her hands deep into her pockets.

So did he. "The 'it'? Truth. Joy. Joy to the world. Peace on earth. Peace of mind. Minor little life details like that." He paused and watched his feet. Within seconds, he lifted his head and smiled. "And the problem you wanted to discuss?"

It might have been her imagination, but the waves almost

looked slushy, as if half-frozen. Maybe it was the way the wind drove them hard, or the way their intensity stirred up sand and rock, turning what landed on the shore into what Aunt Sarah would have described as "gray water"—used bathtub water or sudsless dishwater drained from the kitchen sink post-cleanup.

She'd seen the effect before, along Lakeshore Drive in Chicago last winter, on days when she welcomed the cold as she walked the water's edge, grateful that something mirrored the misery of her broken heart. The waves ached. She wasn't alone. Christmas had been in the air, but she'd gotten her answer. She and Aunt Sarah would share it alone. Again. Think of the money she saved on gifts for her parents and the last two guys who'd bailed on her before the holiday season revved up. And two months after the last breakup, Aunt Sarah moved to Oregon to start a new job.

"Alexis?"

If either love interest had half the personality or integrity of the one who walked beside her right now . . . *How did my thoughts drift so far out to sea?* She turned and walked backward, the red lighthouse standing as straight and unmoving as ever. "Some beacon you turned out to be."

"What?"

She whipped around to walk forward again, toward the far end of the boardwalk. "I meant . . . that . . . I expected to find some answers here."

"It might help if we started talking about the question."

"Cold air is bracing," she began, "but also distracting. All I can think about is a hot mocha or hot apple cider. We're not going to get another Indian summer, are we?" She let her shoulders fall forward to emphasize her disappointment.

"We probably won't see fifty-degree temps or higher until April."

"Such an encourager."

"My third favorite place for brainstorming just happens to have hot apple cider on the menu."

"Let me guess. It also has a butter-yellow leather couch and spells café with two *f*'s?"

"How did you know? Race you back to the van."

"Not fair. Your stride is twice as long as mine." He was already running at full speed.

"But you have that ballet dancer agility," he called over his shoulder.

She had to get back to running. This project had kept her chained to her computer or the job site too much. If Algoma didn't close the boardwalk in the worst of the winter, she could—*Ouch!*

So much for agility.

"Alexis, are you okay?"

"Yeah." Embarrassed. Bordering on mortified. But okay. "Landed funny on my—" *Ow!* Not a good sign. She couldn't use her left arm to push herself upright. "My arm is a little angry with me right now." Alexis held her elbow with her other hand. "It'll get over its mood. I'll be right there."

But she wouldn't. He'd closed the gap between them before she could pull herself off the boardwalk surface without using her hands. *Graceful. Like a ballet dancer . . . who quit lessons too soon.*

"Please tell me you're okay." Gabe looked her over as if she'd endured a bone-crushing tackle rather than slipped on an icy spot. "Head? Knees? Ribs?"

"Gabe, I landed on my elbow. Probably sprained it. That's all. Tennis elbow. That's what I'll call it. Then I can get the athlete-sympathy I've always craved." She pinched her eyes shut. It did nothing to stave off the knife-stabs of pain.

"If you'd wanted the afternoon off, you could have said so." Gabe took her other elbow and walked her toward the van. "You're the boss."

"I may have to deputize you for the remainder of the day." *Pain level from one to ten? Forty.* She fought against a wave of nausea rivaling the surge of Lake Michigan against defenseless sand.

"Hey, if you're going to hurl," Gabe said, "aim that way." He pointed toward the snow-covered grassy slope on the west side of the boardwalk.

She nodded. And obeyed.

CHAPTER TWELVE

"She beat me in arm wrestling, Doc." Gabe scratched his head. "But if you ask me, it wasn't worth it."

The North Shore Medical Clinic doctor shook his head, no doubt familiar with Gabe Langley's sense of humor and its random connection to appropriate timing.

"Pay no attention to that man behind the curtain," Dr. VanNess said, yanking the privacy curtain shut to separate Alexis and her medical team from her good-natured heckler.

"I need to let you know that I"—Alexis tried not to tense as the doctor pressed his thumbs into the flesh above and below her elbow—"can't afford to have an injury slow me down right now. Ouch!"

"We'll get you something for the pain real soon, Ms. Blake. The x-rays show a radial head fracture. Broken elbow."

A voice from behind the curtain said, "I *knew* it." A moment later, "Sorry, Alexis."

"Not as sorry as I am," she called back.

"It's not the worst kind. We see this more than you'd think with falls on the ice. Now, a supracondylar fracture would have required surgery, a cast, and *then* six weeks in a sling."

"I feel so much better about it all now."

"The woman has a bit of a sarcastic edge, Doc."

"Gabe?" Dr. VanNess peeked around the curtain. "I don't need to ask you to wait outside, do I?"

"I'll behave."

When the doctor turned back, Alexis mouthed, "*No, he won't.*"

Dr. VanNess whispered, "Do you want me to—?" and thumbed a "*hit the road, Jack*" motion.

She shook her head and smirked. "He means well."

Dr. VanNess asked her to squeeze his hand. *Misery*. But she could do it.

"How did that feel? Or need I ask?"

"It'll be fine. I'll ice it tonight." *Ironic. I'll ice it because I fell on the ice.*

From behind the curtain, "I'll make sure she does."

"So," Dr. VanNess said, "you can check in on her, Gabe?" Eyebrows raised, he waited for the invisible answer.

Alexis closed her eyes. Not against the pain this time. "He's already caregiving for his father. Can we go now?"

"Did you miss the part about the sling, Ms. Blake? I'll write a prescription for a strong enough pain med to cover you for the next few days. Gabe, can you pick it up for her while we get her—?" His face changed. "Never mind. You can . . . you can take her through the drive-up window when you two leave here."

What was that about? Wouldn't it save time if he—?

Oh. It was probably a narcotic. And Dr. VanNess stopped short of letting Gabe *handle* it for her? A designer couldn't go far without imagination. But sometimes it worked too many hours. Like now. The doctor's hesitation could be as simple as Alexis needing to sign for the medication herself. Or the fact that they weren't a married couple. That was it. As simple as that. The knot in her stomach told her it was something more.

Her heart sank at the sight of the sling. How was she supposed to appear on camera with that marine-blue eyesore? "Does it come in other colors?"

"Like a nice burnt pumpkin?" Gabe asked, the curtain now pulled back.

"Afraid not," the nurse answered. "It's this or black."

"I'll take black," Alexis said, then added, "please."

"I'm afraid industrial blue is all we have in stock right now."

"Fine. Great. Swell."

"I must say"—Gabe shrugged his shoulders—"it brings out the color in your eyes."

"Nice try, Gabe. But I'm not in the mood for fake compliments."

The nurse cradled Alexis's bent arm in the sling. "I don't think it was fake. Nice catch," she whispered.

He's not my catch. He's my cameraman.

"Hold still a little longer for me, will you? This time of year, we add something special to this lovely sling ensemble."

A few minutes later, Alexis exited the exam room with a

prescription in her good hand, a gel ice pack bulging at her elbow, and a holly-trimmed set of jingle bells at the top of her sling.

"Looks festive," Gabe said, following her with their coats. "*Sounds* festive."

Alexis kept walking.

"NOT HAPPY. Nah-ah-ah-aht happy at all. Not happy."

"You mentioned that." Gabe stopped at the drive-through window of the pharmacy and took the prescription from Alexis. He glanced at it a moment, took a deep breath, then stuck it under the spring-loaded breeze bar on the slide-out drawer.

The pharmacy tech looked it over and spoke into a goose-necked microphone. "Have you had this medication in the past, Ms. Blake?"

Alexis leaned toward the window beyond Gabe, but the rods of pain that shot from her elbow to her shoulder forced her back to upright. She couldn't see the tech's face, but said, "No. I haven't."

"And have you filled prescriptions here with us before?"

"No. I'm from out of town."

"Can you send your ID in, please? And your insurance card? And a method of payment?"

She tried to unzip her purse with one hand while using her right-angle arm to hold it steady. "One minute."

"Let me help you," Gabe said, reaching for her purse.

She protected it with both arms.

"You can't afford purse pride, Alexis. Let me help."

Purse pride? She removed her guard and let him unzip her purse and dig out the card wallet she indicated.

"I hate it when you're right," she said. *What made her confess that?*

"Well, you'll have to get used to it. I'm right a lot."

She would have crossed her arms and glared at him, but the sling and discomfort prevented her from that action.

"Unfortunately, I'm wrong a lot, too. And on any given day, it could go either way. So . . . "

When the drive-through drawer opened again, it held a small clipboard with a form for Alexis to sign. Gabe propped the clipboard so she could manage the maneuver. Within minutes, Gabe retrieved a small paper bag from the extended drawer. He handed it to Alexis with two fingers.

"It's not poison, Gabe."

"For some people."

The pharmacy tech let them know the receipt was in the bag and wished them a good day.

Starting when? So far, it's been a tad un-good.

"Take that with plenty of water," Gabe said.

"Yes, Dr. Langley. So the instructions note. So, are you one of those no-medication-ever people? And is there a . . . reason for that?" Maybe too close? She changed tactics. "Would you rather I tried rubbing coconut oil on my broken elbow? Or extract from a geranium?"

Gabe changed his grip on the steering wheel. "Wrong flower."

"What?"

"Let's get you home."

Alexis adjusted the strap of her sling where it rubbed on her neck. "I need to get back to the job site."

"It's not a job site. It's Elsie's home." His voice wasn't unkind, but it held an edge she hadn't heard before.

"What's gotten into you, Gabe? I'm the one in pain, here."

He signaled to pull onto the highway. "Believe me, Alexis. You're not the *only* one."

THE SNOW DRIFTED like goose down in a slow-motion pillow fight. It made more sound than the absence of conversation in the van on the way back to the fieldstone house. Alexis didn't feel like pursuing whatever had set Gabe on edge. She had her own issues. She'd found it hard enough to pull off "perky" on camera. Now perky had to override pain and whatever side effects the medication would have. Not to mention angling every shot to avoid the not-in-the-project's-color-palette sling.

Maybe she could remove it long enough to film the segments they needed.

And maybe pigs could fly.

Oh. Some can.

"There you go," Gabe said. "Your 'job site.'" He put the van in Park and turned off the engine.

"It's beautiful, isn't it? Even unfinished. The stone against the backdrop of snow. That soft turquoise trim. The new back door to match the one on the front. It's a sweet little house."

"It is. I want to do a good job filming this for you. And for Elsie."

"Me, too." Alexis opened and closed her fist. The pill she'd taken in the van on the way hadn't taken effect yet. "You, I'm not worried about, Gabe. It's me."

He turned to face her. "Why would you be worried about your skills?"

"Not my design skills. My listening skills. You were right to point out I hadn't been listening to her. Or to you. I think you were about to tell me something about what scares you, and I shut you off."

He faced what lay past the windshield again. "Someday. Maybe when this is over." He opened the driver's door and was careful not to slam it. She waited while he came to her side of the van. It would take practice, but she was going to have to let people help her if she was to have any chance of completing the project. At the moment, she couldn't even lift a picture frame to position it on a wall. And somehow, she'd tiptoed too close to a darkness that had descended on Gabe.

He opened her door and held out his hand. She slid to the edge of her seat and lowered herself to the ground, leaning hard on the assistance he offered. "That goofy smile of yours?" she said. "Bring it back, please."

He looked at his feet. When he looked up, he said, "Let's show the crew your fancy new arm-wear. I'll wait for your signal when you've had enough and want to go home." He conjured a facsimile of his typical grin.

"That'll do for now."

"You have snowflakes on your eyelashes."

"I do?" She would have had to let go of his arm to wipe them away.

"Leave them. They look good on you."

By the time Alexis had told the story to the work crew and borne more than a few attempts at designer humor, the pain in her elbow had lessened a little but her head was growing fuzzy. She finished the last of the tea Elsie had made on her hotplate in her temporary kitchenette upstairs, gave final instructions to the work crew, and asked Gabe to take her home.

"I like you better like this," Elsie said. "You're more like me."

"What do you mean by that?"

"You have something, too. Something that slows you down. Something you have to explain but don't want to."

Alexis listened. But Elsie said no more.

"The ginger cookies helped, Elsie. Thank you. I shouldn't have taken the med on an empty stomach."

"I'll give you some to take with you." Elsie disappeared

upstairs while Alexis stayed sitting on the top riser of a step stool.

"When will the walls be done, guys?"

Ralph answered. "Living room? Paint and all? Maybe the end of next week. Kitchen? Week after that."

"We're running a day or two behind schedule. And with taking a couple of days off for Thanksgiving next week . . . "

"Are you feeling okay, Alexis?"

"Mmm. Why?"

"You just said, 'Caking a douple of tays off . . . '"

"A little sleepy. That's all. Probably better get home."

"Gabe said he was letting the van warm up for you. I'll get your coat."

"Elsie's bringing me cookies."

"I already did, dear. Right here. In your hand. Ralph, can you and a couple of the men . . . you know . . . hoist her out there?"

"Ryan, get the forklift. She's not going to make it under her own steam."

"I'm not that heavy."

"It was a joke, boss. Now, lean your head on my shoulder and . . . "

CHAPTER THIRTEEN

"Good morning, Sunshine!"

Gabe's voice? No. He must be shouting through a floor vent or something.

Alexis rolled to her side. Wrong move. The wedged pillow prevented her from rolling onto her elbow, but she'd gone far enough to stir another cycle of pain daggers. She held her elbow—with its saggy, diaper-ish thawed ice pack—and slid to the other side of the bed to sit up.

"Breakfast will be ready momentarily. I suggest the patient take care of any morning duties she finds necessary."

It was Gabe. And he was in her apartment. *His* apartment. The one she was borrowing. She didn't have to change out of pajamas. She was wearing what she'd worn yesterday. But she did need to visit the bathroom.

When she emerged, teeth brushed, face washed, and pants as straight as she could get them with only one good arm, she found the table set and Gabe standing at the stove. "How did you get in here? You gave me the key."

"Did you assume I didn't have a spare?" He wiggled his eyebrows. "Don't worry. I borrowed Dad's."

So much for her imagined security system.

"The sun's shining." She padded to the wall of windows, noting that her balance had improved significantly from the day before. "What a sight."

"Isn't it? I waste a lot of time standing at those windows."

"Appreciating a view is never a waste of time."

"She's not only awake, folks, she's a philosopher."

Alexis shuffled back to the table and sat at one of the two place settings.

"How's the pain?"

"Tolerable." She'd chosen a word and she was sticking to it.

Gabe turned, holding a spatula like a microphone. "Would you tell me if it wasn't?"

"I might. In exchange for a cup of coffee."

"Already poured." He slid a mug in front of her.

"A Christmas mug. Thanks a lot."

He tugged it a few inches away from her. "If you're not interested . . . "

"No, please. Need the coffee. It's the Christmas reminder that stings a little. A lot."

"You're worried we won't finish in time."

"Worse than that."

"You're worried I'll add video of your ramblings yesterday on the way home from Elsie's."

Her ears burned as if she'd touched them with her curling iron, which at the moment she couldn't manage with only one working hand. "You didn't."

"Three hundred thousand hits on YouTube so far."

"Gabe, tell me you didn't." *He wouldn't have.*

"I didn't."

"And you're being truthful right now?" Her stomach still did its imitation of a tap dance.

He plated a perfect omelet, sprinkled scallions on top, and set it before her. "Drink your coffee before it gets cold, boss."

"What's in this omelet? It looks delicious."

"Morels. I had to use the freeze-dried kind, since they're obviously not in season right now."

"Obviously."

"Stinging nettle cheese."

"What?"

"It's delicious. One of these days I'll take you to the specialty cheese shop in Egg Harbor that carries it. And grilled asparagus."

"You grilled asparagus this morning? Seriously. You started up the barbeque grill and—"

"Smell." He tugged his shirtsleeve to a peak and held it under her nose.

"Gabe, I'm not going to . . . "

"Go ahead. Sniff."

"Smells like bitter cold, a crisp clean winter morning . . . and grilled meat."

"Garlic chicken. That's for supper. Thought I'd plan ahead. Do you have a headache?"

Alexis stopped pinching the bridge of her nose. "You're not average, are you, Gabe?"

"Ooh. Average. Not my favorite word." He grabbed another plate from the microwave and sat across from her.

"You made *your* omelet first?"

"I always make two and give away the one that turns out the best. Sure you don't have a headache?"

"Way past time for my pain medicine. Must have it now." She held her shoulder. Holding her elbow would hurt like crazy.

She watched his face change—as radically as the difference between flattering and unflattering lighting. So, she had indeed discovered his kryptonite. "But I thought I might try ibuprofen this time."

The light returned.

"I don't like how the other stuff makes me feel inside," she said.

"I did. Way too much."

Kryptonite. "Do you want to tell me about it?"

He peeked into her coffee mug. "Need a refill? I do." Gabe stood and grabbed the half-full clear carafe. He couldn't hide that his eyes darted to the corner, where the darkened Christmas tree stood.

"Gabe, I won't press you."

"You have a right to know. Some would say I should have

told you before you hired me." After he'd refilled their coffees, he crossed the room to the tree and adjusted one of the ornaments that, from his own account, had remained untouched for almost a year.

She took a bite of her omelet and prayed he'd have strength to say what he had to say and that she'd have wisdom to respond with grace. Or support. Or understanding. Whatever he needed.

"We don't all get addicted to painkillers," he said, still holding the ornament. "Only one in four, they say. *Only* one in four." He rejoined her at the table, but left his fork where it lay. "I'm, to use your words, not average."

"You didn't even want to touch the paper bag my medication came in yesterday."

Elbow on the table, he propped his chin in the heel of his hand. "A little extreme, maybe, but I promised myself, my mom, and my God that I wouldn't touch it again. I mean to keep my word."

"How long have you been clean?"

"I express it a little differently. How long have I been *free?* Long enough to know it's possible. Short enough to know not to let down my guard." He sipped his coffee.

How long is long enough? My parents promised, too. The ache in her arm intensified, as if it knew it wasn't going to get what it craved.

"Random drug screenings?" He didn't look her in the eye.

"What about them?"

"Is that what you'd like me to do? It can be arranged through Dr. VanNess. We've been through this before."

She rubbed her upper arm. Thorns and needles and knife blades tore through her nerve endings. "I don't want that."

"So it's . . . " Gabe caught her gaze for a moment, then looked away. "My job is over?"

"I don't know where we stand right now, Gabe. But if we can't finish this project, it won't be because of you. It'll be because of me." She lifted her slinged arm six inches, which turned out to be five and a half inches too much.

THANKSGIVING HAD COME and gone by the time Alexis felt up to asking Gabe to take her to Elsie's. The work had gone on without her, evidenced by Gabe's frequent video calls. Each of the crew members popped onto the screen to wish her well and assure her that everything was as close to on schedule as possible, given the hiccups an older home could muster. If they stayed on task, they could have their end of the work done five days before Christmas Eve and allow her plenty of time to arrange furniture, "fuss" with the details, and decorate for the holiday finale meal.

Five days. Not a lot of time. And judging from the progress she'd made so far, she wouldn't be moving couches by herself when the time came, as she normally did.

"You're sure about this?" Gabe asked when she met him at the top of the stairs, laptop case slung over her good shoulder.

"I don't know how your dad keeps his sanity, confined to the house all the time. I have to go somewhere. Do something."

"To his credit, Dad likes naps a lot more than you do. He's quite good at it. But I can tell he's going a little stir-crazy, too. He's healing, but so slowly. I like your hat."

"One-armed hair styling demands hats."

"Do you want me to try to—?"

"No!"

"I was going to say that I could find a hair stylist who could come to the house."

"Oh. When we start filming again, that might be my only answer."

Gabe—once again—helped her into the van and took his place behind the wheel. "I plan to work in some scenes today, if you're up to it. I like the challenge of our camouflaging your bright blue sling. You can peek from behind a doorway. Have a swatch of upholstery fabric draped over your shoulder. Pretend you're holding up a piece of reclaimed wood."

"I'm wearing a hat."

"Which the audience will find charming. Yeah, do that," he said. "Pull out some tufts of hair to frame your face. That's good."

"Tufts of hair. Very elephant-like."

"Alexis, your mirror has been lying to you if it's told you you're not a beautiful woman. Even in a hat."

Well. "You might want to try one, too, Gabe."

"I'm *wearing* a hat."

"One with longer ear pieces. Your ears are beet red."

He tilted his chin. "From the extreme cold."

"If you say so."

The approach to the house stole Alexis's breath. The snow-covered land surrounding it, as smooth as expert fondant on a wedding cake. The creek, still moving, but hemmed in scalloped ice. The stone bridge. The woods on either side made it feel even more secluded than it was. And the fieldstone exterior of the house spoke of landowners hand-selecting the right stones from among the thousands that littered the fields and woods at a time when it would have been more efficient to use Cream City brick. The stories that house could tell. Stories Alexis would likely never hear.

The trim, door, and shutters, with their subtle egg-blue, set the stone house off so beautifully, Alexis wished it had been her idea.

"Are you inspired?" Gabe asked. "You're very quiet."

"I've missed this place. I care about it, and about how Elsie will feel about it when we're done."

"It won't be long until we find out. We could probably get some outdoor greenery hung today or tomorrow. Storms are predicted for later in the week. Any of the preliminary camera-work I can finish before the rush at the end will help."

He drew the van behind the house and parked among the construction crew vehicles, as always. He hurried to help her from the van, as always. This time felt different. She wasn't sure why.

Until she walked through the back door.

"This is almost a real kitchen!"

"Hey, boss lady. Welcome back."

"Guys, this looks just beautiful. I'm so impressed."

Ralph dusted off a stool with a rag from his back pocket. "Sit. Sit. We'll show you what we've done."

"I don't have to sit just yet. Oh, the island. I love it. Can I take a peek at the top?"

"Sure," Ralph said, pulling aside the layer of protective cardboard. "Who woulda knowed them boards were once lanes of a bowling alley?"

"I'm stunned. This is really, really gorgeous. The dark stain looks so rich."

Gabe set his first load of camera equipment in the corner. "Your idea about making the vertical surfaces of the island the same color as the exterior trim? A brilliant move. Ties it all together."

"Where's Elsie? I'd love to get her thoughts."

"Went to visit her dad," Ralph said. "Such a tragic story, huh? He don't recognize her. Don't know who she is. But I guess he's pleasant enough. Just don't have no clue she's his daughter."

"Did you know him, Ralph? Before? You've been part of the community for a long time."

"Kept to himself. Seen him a few times back a ways, always with Elsie."

The answers would not come easily. That was clearer every day.

"Don't let me hold you up, crew. You're doing a great job."

"Wander in by the fireplace. I think it turned out good," Ralph said, locking a battery pack onto his portable drill. "Darrell, shoo that cat out. He don't belong in here."

"I think it's a she."

"Either way."

"My fault," Gabe said. "I'll get her. I must not have pulled the door shut when I came in."

If Alexis had two working arms, she would have hugged the fireplace. With the island at one end of the long, open expanse, and the reimagined, converted fireplace at the other—as close to real-looking as they could have made it in light of their inability to get the original working again—she could envision a dozen furniture placement ideas. Elsie insisted on not "cluttering up" the place with too much furniture, which suited Alexis. She might even shift her plan so Christmas dinner could be served in front of the fire.

"Do that again," Gabe said.

"Do what?"

"Lean against the mantel, looking up at the ceiling. The lighting is perfect for . . . this. Now, let your line of sight trace down to the fire with that same expression of appreciation on your face. Good. Aw, that's good."

"How are you going to hide my sling?"

"You did. You haven't taken off your coat. It looks like you draped it over one shoulder like a film noir detective might have in the thirties or forties. Sophisticated and mysterious."

"That is so not in keeping with our theme, Gabe."

"We have a theme?"

"*Restoring Christmas?*"

"Oh, yeah. That."

CHAPTER FOURTEEN

She had no choice.

Alexis listened to the Christmas mood music play on her phone—"Still, Still, Still"—while she struggled to make sense of her hair. Washing it in the shower hadn't been nearly as hard as trying to go hatless for the day's taping. She laughed at the oddity of such soothing music when the scene in her borrowed bathroom looked more like the inside of a scientist's wind tunnel.

No choice. Having one arm out of commission meant she had to cut the music and use the phone to text Gabe.

Within minutes, he stood at the base of the stairs, wielding a tree branch lopper, a garden rake, and a can of WD40. "You need help with your hair?"

He'd done it again—found a way to turn what could have been embarrassing into a comedy routine that broke the blister so healing could start. "I couldn't think of anyone else to call. I should have thought harder. My hair doesn't need to be lopped. Or raked. I just need it put in a ponytail or something."

Gabe set aside the garden tools and stood behind the kitchen chair where she sat. One by one, he picked up the items she'd arranged on the table—her brush, hair spray, a small mirror, and a curling iron.

"Stylist to the stars Gabriel Langley . . . cannot work with these!" His affected French accent eased her tension even more.

"A simple ponytail, please?"

"What? Your arm brrrroken?" This time he sounded more like a Greek mother. "Oh. My apologies."

"Don't have all day. I'm"—Alexis didn't claim to have his wit, but she could play along—"meeting an Addy Award winner for coffee in a few moments. We'll be spending the day together on what could be the launch of my own television series."

Gabe pulled the brush through her hair. "Really?" Back to himself again. "Did you tell me that before? I thought this was all for the one Christmas special. I mean, it will be great for your career . . . "

She tilted the mirror so she could see his face. "I haven't made a big deal about it, because the chances are so slim. Who am I to think that—? Ouch! Have you ever brushed long hair before?"

He took a step back. "You dare doubt my skill, mademoiselle?"

"The time, Gabe?"

"Ah, yes. Your appointment with the world-renowned

videographer. I've heard of his work. And, for your information, I wore my hair at least that long a few years ago."

"You did?"

"Let's just say it wasn't my best look. Although it was as silky as a . . . as . . . silk."

"Could we hurry this up? I found a few treasures at one of the antique shops here in town yesterday on my wild first-time-driving-one-armed adventure. But I hoped to stop at the secondhand store to look for a few more copper items I can repurpose into ornaments for Elsie's tree before we go out to the house."

He continued brushing.

Wish we didn't have to hurry.

"Do you have a name for the house?" Gabe asked, reaching for a hair tie. "The Heart-and-Home shows I've watched in the last couple of weeks all have names for the houses designers work on. The Fernwood Cottage. The Mountainview Estate. The House of Eight Gables."

"Seven."

"You saw that episode?"

"It's a Nathaniel Hawthorne story."

"Right. The point is, shouldn't Elsie's house have a heartwarming name? Elsie's Place sounds like a burger joint."

"Not a bad idea, Gabe."

He shielded her eyes and spritzed hair spray on whatever it was he'd done with her hair. "And . . . *voilà!* Perfec-shee-own!"

She risked looking in the mirror. "Gabe, this is . . . great."

"You seem surprised, mademoiselle. I would call it a man-bun, but you're . . . like . . . not. A man."

"Yes, I caught that. Thank you. It's much better than I could have done. Especially one-armed."

"Any time."

"Thank you." *Gabe, Gabe, Gabe. You are so different from most men I've known.*

"Ready to go? Need your ice pack or . . . or anything?"

Time to talk. "I want you to know I disposed of my high-powered painkillers."

Facing him now, she could see the flash of concern that shot across his face.

"Why would you do that, Alexis? You might need them."

She knew the war he waged inside. Part of it, anyway. She'd battled the argument, too. With the grip substances held on her parents, a grip that pulled them into an endlessly spiraling abyss, she'd been hesitant to take even vitamin supplements until Aunt Sarah walked her through the difference between using and Using. The difference between "as prescribed" and "as craved." She couldn't live their fears for them, couldn't let their demons invade her dreams.

"They're a legitimate answer for some people, Alexis. Not a threat, if used like they should be." His last words disappeared into his chest.

"But *you* don't need me to have them around. That was enough. The discomfort is tolerable. I might have leaned on the pills just because I had them. You helped remind me there's a time and a place for most things. And sometimes, enduring is better than numbing. Sometimes."

"Can I quote you?"

"No, but you can warm up the van. I'll be ready in ten minutes."

SHIVERS SHOT THROUGH Alexis's nerve endings. The good kind of shiver. Sitting right in front of her near the faux fireplace on the well-worn showroom floor of the 2nd Hand Rose thrift shop was Elsie's couch! The one Alexis imagined for her. She had one ordered from a traditional supplier, but it wasn't THE one. This was it.

Alexis ran her hand along the antique hand-carving along the curved back of the sofa and over the plush upholstery on the arms and cushions. The perfect shade of heirloom tomato-red to use as a statement piece in Elsie's living area. The pop of color the room needed. With a hint of coppery dark maple in the wood accents.

"May I take a picture of this to show my client?" she asked the sweatered manager of the shop. "On second thought, I'll do that, but I'm going to pay for it now. I'm sure she'll fall in love like I did."

They negotiated an equitable price. Alexis thumb-texted Gabe that she was ready to go—and would he mind hoisting a sofa, by himself, into the back end of the van? He appeared from the back of the shop with his own treasures—a 1950s Kodak Brownie camera in one hand and his fingers laced with a half-dozen copper cookie cutters.

"The camera?" Alexis asked.

"For Dad." He dumped the cookie cutters on the check-out counter. "He has a collection of old camera equipment at his shop."

"I've never seen his place of business."

"I'll have to take you over there someday. It's on Clark Street."

Someday. She'd be a "resident" of Algoma for less than three more weeks. Three very full, crazy, devoted weeks. Watching Gabe hand her the small bag of purchases while he tested his ability to handle the sofa single-handedly made the weeks seem like a timer she couldn't defuse before it exploded and flattened all that had come to life since she'd arrived.

Enough of the drama, Alexis. You have a job to do.

IN THE END, Gabe had to enlist the aid of a friend who worked at a car repair shop a few blocks away in order to get the sweet-looking but big-boned sofa into the back of the van, after repositioning several pieces of expensive camera equipment.

"You're sure she's going to love it?" he said after high-fiving his friend and promising to catch up with him soon.

Alexis pulled her coat across the sling and tried buttoning the second button to keep it from slipping off. She'd become agile enough to manage other buttons with only her right hand. This one challenged her.

Gabe took over. "Better?"

"Yes. Thank you. And I long for her to love it. Not sure, but hopeful."

"Hopeful is good. We'll go with that." He helped her into the van. "But, it might be beneficial if we have her take a look at it before we bring it into the house."

"That heavy, huh?"

"They built them well in those days."

The trip out to the property flew by as she pondered how best to convince Elsie to let Alexis keep the sofa. For Elsie. Forever.

The designer's dilemma. The work he or she created remained someone else's to live with . . . or change.

Ralph's Abel-Bodied team couldn't arrive until noon because most of them also served as volunteer firefighters for the village of Algoma and couldn't miss the morning's safety training session. So Gabe and Alexis were the first to arrive.

"Elsie's car is gone, Alexis."

"Again? Where does she go?"

Gabe let out a noisy exhale. "I don't think I can maneuver the camera equipment out with that sofa back there."

"Maybe she went to visit her dad at the long-term care center."

"Doubtful. Look. It snowed all night. No tracks. She must have left shortly after we did late yesterday afternoon."

The muscles across the back of her shoulders tightened. Worry sat heavily in her stomach. "Why won't she tell us where she's been going? Why all the secrecy? I don't get it. Maybe we should try to contact her family. This could be serious." Family history of dementia. Elsie expressed her own concerns about its possibility. Shouldn't her sons get involved, no matter what had estranged them until now?

"More importantly, who feeds her chickens and goats when she's gone?"

She cast a sideways glance at the man within punching distance, but only with her bad arm.

"A reasonable question," Gabe said.

"She told us that first day that she has her friend feed her animals when she's gone, the friend who submitted her"— why hadn't they thought of that before?—"name for the contest. Maybe we can hide out in the chicken coop until the woman shows up, and pump her for information about Elsie's clandestine operations."

"Your elbow is really hurting you, huh? Making you a little delirious?"

Alexis might have to consider a modified version of that plan. "Maybe she left a note."

"She never does anymore. Ooh. New Christmas song for the occasion. 'No shepherds watched her flocks by night.'"

Sitting in the idle van wouldn't accomplish anything. Nor would inventing twisted versions of carols for this curious Christmas season. Maybe there was something they could make progress on—like touching up the trim on the re-glazed windows inside the house while they waited for Ralph's crew or Elsie's return, or both.

Gabe unlocked the back door of the fieldstone house while Alexis stomped snow from her feet. As soon as the door opened, a dark, ankle-tall figure scooted out the door.

"Look out!"

Alexis backpedaled a few steps to stay out of its way. Elsie's barn cat, Tabitha. She looked like she'd had a long, miserable bath. "How did the cat get in there? And when?"

"Larger question," Gabe said. "Where did all this water come from?"

CHAPTER FIFTEEN

"I GOT THE WATER VALVE SHUT OFF under the bathroom sink," Alexis said, wiping her hand on her pant leg.

"How did you manage that with one working arm?" Gabe swept another wave of standing water out the back door and away from the short sidewalk approach.

"Desperate times call for desperate measures."

He raised the broom handle high. "*Extremis malis extrema remedia.*"

"What have you been reading?"

"Sixteenth-century literature. Just for fun." He sloshed another swipe with the carpenter's broom. "I'm switching to the shop vac now."

"Let me run the shop vac," Alexis said. "I can do that with one hand."

"What a mess. The water must have been running most of the night. How did that happen?"

Alexis hollered over the roar of the shop vac, "The crew knows not to leave the sink plunger depressed. When the water got bumped on, it was too much for the porcelator."

"The what?" Gabe hollered back.

"That little hole in the sink for overflow."

"Only a designer would know what that's called."

"Or a plumber."

"Which we could use right about now."

One thing at a time. One thing at a time. You can assess damage after the water's cleaned up. Good theory. Almost impossible to follow as she steered the nozzle of the shop vac toward cabinet bases and over the once beautifully refinished hardwood floor. Her tower of cardboard boxes leaned dramatically to the south. The lower boxes were soaked, no longer stable. How much of what had been shipped inside was ruined?

One thing at a time.

She switched off the shop vac. The action brought a measure of sound relief, but no emotional benefit. Like picking through the wreckage after an explosion, Gabe and Alexis walked the rooms of the main floor.

"Remember when you said you wanted to leave the 'charming' slant to the floors, Alexis?"

She nodded.

"Smart move. The water didn't make it all the way to the fireplace. It pooled there in the kitchen and bathroom."

"Where all the expensive stuff is." Aunt Sarah told her she'd been one of those babies who'd refused a pacifier. She wouldn't have turned it down now. Nothing about the sight she surveyed seemed comforting.

"Oh, this is encouraging." Gabe apparently disagreed.

What had he found?

"I think the kitchen island escaped damage."

Alexis put a damp hand over her heart to keep it from pounding so hard. One little ray of hope. "The wheels?"

"They kept it out of harm's way, just by inches, it looks like, judging from the waterline on the other cabinets."

"The waterline on other cabinets. Not what I want to hear at this stage of the restoration."

Gabe tapped the former bowling alley top of the island. "Focus here. You saved the island with your insistence on making it movable with the locking wheels. Yay for you."

"And I also insisted Elsie would love the no-touch sensor faucets for the bathroom and kitchen. She was happy with an outhouse. I pushed for no-touch sensors."

"She'll appreciate that when her hands are full of hamburger grease one day."

"If Elsie had been here last night, she would have heard the water running and stopped it before it got this bad."

Gabe moved a cardboard box from the stack to the top of the island. "I blame the cat."

"I'm not *blaming* Elsie. I don't expect her to stay home for the rest of her life."

"No, really. I blame the cat. I think the cat did it." He smirked.

Funny how fast Gabe could switch between encouraging and irritating. "Gabe, your theory is that the cat snuck in under cover of darkness, closed the sink plunger, and thought,

'Now, how can I cause the most havoc this fine evening? I know, I'll turn on the water full force and watch the humans panic in the morning'?"

"Exactly. Except for the intentionality part. Although one can never tell with a cat. Want me to get any of this destruction on video? Wish I'd thought of that earlier. I'm off my feed."

"No!"

"Yes, I am. I usually have a snack about this time in the morning. It helps keep me from wild blood-sugar swings."

"Gabe, honestly!" The house wasn't large enough to escape his presence, but she put as much distance between them as she could. The living room stood only half soaked, the floor a darker color of wood where it had marinated in water all night. One lone folding chair sat near the fireplace. She swirled around to face the worst of the mess and her temporary nemesis. "Gabe, I can't even find a place to fling myself in utter distress! And yes, I realize that sounded extreme. What *is* that?"

"Whining. I thought it was you."

"I'm . . . over . . . here. The sound is coming from . . . the bathroom."

Her fractured elbow didn't keep her from running to investigate, Gabe on her heels.

In Alexis's—or Elsie's—beautiful hammered copper sink sat Tabitha, slapping at the now-inactive faucet.

"How did that cat get in again?"

Alexis narrowed her eyes. "Larger question. Can you sue a cat for damages?"

When Ralph's crew arrived, they joined the damage assessment team, agreeing with Alexis that it was pure wonder some items were untouched or needed minimal repair.

"But these lower cabinets . . ." Ralph said, kicking at the toe-plate they'd installed the day before.

"I know."

"And the floor. That don't look good."

"The floor." Alexis had avoided saying it out loud until now. They'd have to replace all the flooring, maybe the subfloor, too. Dollars and time they didn't have.

Gabe added, "I took care of the cat."

All eyes widened. "Dare I ask how?" Alexis closed her eyes for the answer.

"Not a long-term solution, but I found an old feed barrel in the barn. I put chicken wire over the open end and laid it on its side."

"I don't understand how it keeps getting in the house," Alexis said. "We've been more cautious than normal about that."

Gabe stepped closer. "The larger question is—"

"Gabe, we have to stop coming up with larger and more important questions."

"—why do I hear water dripping?"

The room quieted.

"You got good ears, Gabe," Ralph said. "Follow me to the basement, men." He headed outside.

"And woman," Gabe added.

"If she don't mind the cobwebs and such. Most fieldstone basements around here aren't pretty things like you see in magazines."

"Or on television shows," Alexis added, gesturing for Gabe to put away the camera he'd shouldered.

"Please, please, please let me film this," he said. "I'll edit it out later, if you insist."

She exhaled like a whale breaching the surface of the ocean. "At least my hair looks nice."

"Or . . . it did. Before all . . . this."

"Always the encourager, Gabe Langley. Always the encourager."

The basement could only be accessed from a storm door outside. They all donned coats. The work crew grabbed heavy-duty flashlights and led the way down the steep concrete steps.

Alexis didn't have any trouble with the low ceiling joists, but the other men alternately ducked and clunked their heads on pipes and low-hanging rafters until they adopted what looked like a horribly uncomfortable posture. Gabe seemed especially miserable in that stance.

Flashlights sweeping the cavern found a newer model furnace in one corner, an old wooden high chair, a seen-better-days crib, and a set of shelves filled with glistening home-canned products—peaches, green beans, beets, apples, carrots . . .

"That's impressive, right there," Ralph said. "I know where I'm coming next time there's a tornado warning."

"The water, Ralph?" Alexis could only search where the flashlight illuminated a small circle. But the floor underneath them seemed dry.

"This might help," Gabe said. Faint but welcome light flooded the basement when he pulled a chain connected to a single light bulb between rafters.

"Well, there you go, then," Ralph said, his flashlight—still needed—trained on a place high on the west wall where a slow trickle of wetness followed the jagged path of stones and ancient mortar like a halfhearted waterfall.

"Where's that coming from?" Camera now waist height because it couldn't be shouldered in that height-challenged space, Gabe followed Ralph and one of his crew members to the wall.

Ralph scraped at the mortar with the claw part of his hammer. A shower of sand raced the water to the cement floor. "What we have here, people, is a problem."

Alexis envisioned her credit card bill starting to smoke.

"We got your foundation failure, but only in this one spot. Not hard to fix. Give us an hour or so. But we got to find out where the water's coming from. It's too cold out there for this to be snow thaw."

The tiny red alert light on Gabe's camera—that indicates recording—went dark. "I may have an explanation. Can anyone over five foot be excused to go topside?"

"That's all of us, Gabe," Alexis said.

"Good idea." He started up the steps. The rest followed. He stopped near the northwest corner of the house. "That's where I dumped the water from the shop vac," he said, head bowed and finger pointing.

"Guess we know the source of the water, then." Ralph followed the man-made river from a pool of melted snow to the foundation. "Thanks, Gabe. Without that little *foo poh* of yours, we wouldna found the missing rock. Saved a bigger problem."

"Once you're done congratulating one another, could we get back to restoring what's been damaged?" Alexis bit her tongue. Far, far too hard.

"Hmm. And Christmas shows up again," Gabe said, spreading his arms wide. "Restoring what's been damaged—the human-God connection. So God sends the answer in His Son."

"Weekday preacher?" Alexis now couldn't keep the smile from her face. What would she have done if she'd been handed any different crew than this one, any videographer other than Gabe? George would have done an admirable job, no doubt. But Gabe . . .

"Alexis, come to the hayloft with me?"

That's not what I meant.

"Board meeting. Ralph, you too. I think I found an answer."

"To which question?" Alexis mentally scrolled through the ever-growing list.

Gabe turned to walk backward to the barn while Ralph provided Alexis with a stabilizing arm. "The 'What are we going to do about the floors?' question. Have you seen how much square footage of reclaimable wood is right now an unused hayloft?"

"Elsie gonna let you tear it out?" Ralph followed his question with an "Mmm-mmm-mmm."

"Gabe, Elsie's ready to bolt at the next opportunity. How can we ask her to let us tear out the hayloft?"

"Not all of it. Part of it. And . . . she said we could use whatever we wanted out of the barn."

"She meant *items*, Gabe. Not rafters."

"Now, there's an idea."

CHAPTER SIXTEEN

WHETHER OR NOT ELSIE AGREED to dismantling the hayloft, the hardwood floor in the house could not be salvaged. And the subfloor in the kitchen didn't survive the cat flood, either. Each new snowflake that drifted past the window reminded Alexis that D-day drew closer at lightning speed. C-day. Christmas.

Next year, no matter where she stood, career-wise, she'd approach the holiday at a slower pace. Even if she was in the middle of the launch celebration for the *Restoring Christmas* special. This year, Christmas was a date on the calendar and an opportunity.

A date and an opportunity.

She hadn't expected to tear up as she fingered the manger from the papier-mâché nativity set salvaged from the soaked boxes. None of the other pieces had survived. They lay mis-shapen and unusable in the big plastic garbage can.

She could reorder the set, or one that was similar. But at the moment, that seemed as much "second best" as waiting a year to embrace the significance of the season.

Gabe was days away from the anniversary of his mother's death. But, except for his avoidance of the unlit Christmas tree in his/her downstairs apartment, he seemed connected to the spot where his faith and Christmas intersected.

She set the manger in the windowsill. Empty. The Christ Child hadn't made it.

But He did. Maybe that's the point.

"Alexis, what's going on here?"

"Elsie, you're home. Finally. We had a setback." Gabe called it a *cat-astrophe*, but Alexis wasn't about to use that term with the home owner and lover of said cat.

"My . . . house."

A twinge started at Alexis's neck and didn't stop until it got to her ankles. The look on that poor woman's face . . . "Elsie, trust me, the men are putting it back together as we speak. They're making good progress. They've gone to Sturgeon Bay to get more materials to replace the subfloor. Gabe is taking measurements in the barn for— We need to talk."

"Yes. We do." Elsie surveyed the rooms that were in worse shape than when she'd left. "What's this?"

"That"—*Gabe, where are you? We're about to have an emotionally gripping moment that needs to be on the video*—"is your new sofa."

"Old sofa." Elsie eyed it as if it were an interloper on her property.

"Well, yes. An antique. Don't you love it? It's perfect. We had to put it close to the fireplace for now, since this other half

of the living area was damaged in the

you about momentarily."

"You thought I would like this?"

Elsie, I don't know what I can do to pleas

it at a resale shop downtown and it seemed

a different couch on order. Unless I cancel it, i

two or three business days." She waited for Elsie to

didn't. "I can see if the store owner would conside

it back from me. Or I can try to sell it on eBay or Cra

if you're that unhappy with it." Every new word she s

brought tears closer to the surface. Who was she as a design

if she couldn't find her client one element that brought a smile

to her face?

Elsie clutched her hands in front of her. "It can stay."

She skirted around Alexis and planted her feet on the land-

ing to the stairs, then stopped. "It was my father's. Before he

sold it."

"ALEXIS?"

"In here, Gabe." She should sit up. But lying on her side

with her back pressed against the plush upholstery of the sofa

was the most comfortable she'd been since her fall.

"Where?"

She couldn't lift her left arm to wave over the top of the

sofa back so he could see her. The sling and potential pain

prevented that. And she didn't want to wake Elsie by raising

ʋice, so she lifted her left leg in makeshift sign language
Right here."

"What happened? Are you okay? I saw Elsie's car and
ʒought we could talk to her about the loft. Aren't you feeling
ʋell? Is it your elbow?"

"My heart."

"Don't joke about a thing like that." He sat on the sofa
near her feet. "What is it?"

"My heart feels a tiny little bit of joy."

"Um, good. I mean, compared to *no* joy, that's good.
Compared to a *normal* amount of joy, that's . . . "

"This sofa belonged to Elsie's father."

"Really? What was it doing in the resale shop? She doesn't
like it?"

"No. She does. I think. I think our bringing it here made
her . . . happy?" She left the declarative sentence sounding like
a question. Or uncertainty. Both of which it was.

"And that put you in the fetal position."

"It made me love this piece of furniture all the more."
She swung her feet to the floor and pushed herself upright
with her one functioning hand. "The thought of affecting her
happiness is so fulfilling. That brief moment meant so much
to me."

Gabe rubbed the backs of her shoulders. "And that's the
key to good design. Right there."

"You took extra semesters of psychology in college, didn't
you, Gabe?"

"A couple. Maybe. Or four. Why?"

Alexis stared into the unlit fireplace. "It's part of what makes you who you are." She turned and kissed him on the cheek.

Less than three weeks until Christmas. She'd spend every minute of that time regretting what she'd just done.

Almost every minute.

ALEXIS MANAGED TO STAY busy digging through what could be salvaged and what had to be discarded, reordered, or dropped from her list of must-haves as she dug through the rest of the cardboard boxes. Gabe had disappeared again, which kept her from having to apologize.

I shouldn't have to apologize for a simple, innocuous kiss on the cheek. So I won't. No, I have to. Maybe he didn't notice. He had to have noticed. I should just apologize and get it over with.

From opposite ends of the house, Elsie and Gabe entered the kitchen within seconds of one another.

"How was your nap, Elsie?" Gabe asked, grabbing a bottle of water from the small cooler on the corner of the island. His face and hands looked like he'd emerged from a twelve-hour shift in a coal mine.

"I *call* them naps," Elsie said. "Sometimes I don't sleep. I . . . listen."

Alexis's elbow spasmed.

Gabe glanced at Alexis but directed his words to the home owner. "Alexis wants to ask you a question."

Nice one. "I think Gabe would do a *much* better job describing his proposal. His . . . idea."

"Our idea," he said.

Alexis held her hand to him, palm up, giving him the stage.

"Your barn is near the end of its life span."

Psychology 201? Try again, Gabe.

"I'm aware of that," Elsie said. "It's a race to see who topples first. Me or it."

Somehow, her father's longevity had lulled Alexis into assuming Elsie had another quarter century in her. Reality hit with the sharpness of a kidney stone.

"We have an idea for how we can kill two birds, I mean, how we can reclaim at least part of the barn and give it new life." Gabe's face flushed. Under all that coal dust.

"Go on."

Alexis stepped closer to where Gabe stood, in case he needed the support. Or she did.

"We have to replace these original floors."

The set of Elsie's mouth spoke volumes. The news affected her on a level no one else in the room could imagine, no doubt. Alexis tried. She sympathized. She couldn't empathize.

"How did this happen?"

Gabe tapped his fingertips together. He opened his mouth. Nothing came out.

"Elsie," Alexis said, "it was an unfortunate series of events none of us could have predicted. The bathroom sink was inadvertently plugged—"

"No, I think the cat *intended* to—" Gabe closed his mouth.

"As I was saying"—she interrupted before he could create more drama than necessary—"water ran through the night, we believe, and flooded the floors, damaged the base cabinets enough that we have to replace them or risk a mold issue later on."

"So we were wondering," Gabe said, "if it would help cushion the loss of these beautiful floors, and help with the budget Alexis has to work with, if we tore out the flooring in the hayloft and repurposed that wood here in the house. We'd sand off the years of filth—"

"The years of hay dust accumulation, the surface wear." Alexis considered paying for a couple more semesters of psychology instruction for her videographer.

Elsie lifted her chin as she often did when contemplating.

"The wood is in remarkable shape," Gabe said. "And the loft is large enough that we could salvage everything we need for these repairs."

"We're so sorry this happened, Elsie. But it would be kind of heartwarming—wouldn't it? -to see that hayloft reborn here in the kitchen and living room?"

Five seconds of silence. Ten. "My father used to retreat to the hayloft when he needed time to think. Even at eighty years old, he was climbing that ladder. Until I knew what was going on in his mind, I thought he was trying to get away from me. When I took away the ladder—for his protection, mind you—he pouted for weeks." She looked directly at Alexis. "Not that I know anything about that kind of behavior." A faint smile animated the lines on the older woman's face.

"There's a stairway in the barn now," Gabe said. "With handrails."

"Had it built for him. Made it easier on both of us." Elsie ran her foot along one of the warped floorboards that hadn't yet been removed. "If his mind was alert, he'd probably like knowing his hayloft had been put to good use." She lifted her chin again. "I'm going to check on the chickens."

"I'll go with you," Gabe said. "Your cat is in quarantine at the moment and I should explain why."

CHAPTER SEVENTEEN

"Gabe, with all the delays, and my arm, and you being needed for tasks not related to camera work, are we going to have enough footage? I've been trying to map out the script with our adjustments and using the clips you've already edited, but it's not coming together smoothly. Trying not to worry, but . . . " She couldn't fault him for stepping in as a rescuer, but he'd been hired for the video end of things. Not as project manager. Not as comic relief. Not as confidante. Not as superhero.

She'd voiced her battery of questions to the unanswering hayloft. He was up there somewhere. The work crew had enough to do tearing out the last of the base cabinets and finishing the subfloor replacement. For some reason, the hayloft project had captured Gabe's attention. Alexis needed to rein him in and make some sense of their constantly reordered video schedule. The Abel-Bodied men would handle dismantling the floor of the loft.

"Gabe. Can you hear me?"

She'd read enough Laura Ingalls Wilder books to know

that a barn can be surprisingly warm in the winter. If it's filled with heat-radiating animals. When it's close to demolition and this empty, a barn could be a magnet for drafts and shivers.

"Gabe!"

"Alexis. You have to come up here."

He wasn't hired as project manager. Or boss. "Why?"

"You have to see it."

"Gabe, we have work to do."

"This will help."

"You promise?" She'd started climbing the stairs without waiting for Gabe to answer. *Good grief, I'm an enabler. I'm enabling him.*

It wasn't that she was afraid of heights, but her sling made her feel unbalanced, like a seagull with a broken wing trying not to look awkward. She climbed the stairs at what would have been a sluggish pace if she was whole. Without looking down, when she reached the top of the stairs, she stood still and reoriented herself to the hayloft space.

Wider and longer than she thought. Cluttered in spots with the kinds of things other people would store in attics. But if it held any hay, she couldn't see it from where she stood.

"Over here," Gabe called from—of course—the farthest, darkest, cobwebbiest back corner. A window high on the gabled end of the barn shed some light. *Not enough.*

She wrapped her scarf around her neck as many times as its length would allow to add protection against the December

164

temperatures. The flooring underfoot felt solid. No wonder Gabe saw potential in it. Wide planks. Little foot traffic over the years, except from the small creatures Alexis chose not to think about. *Yet I just did.*

If they'd quit making scratchy, scurrying noises, it would be easier to forget they were there.

She found Gabe sitting cross-legged on the floor, with an army-green metal box opened in his lap. "What's in there?"

"Take a look." He handed her a full color snapshot.

Elsie's house. No, the surroundings looked a little different. And the outbuildings. The approach to the house crossed the creek on the opposite side. A small fieldstone building, likely a springhouse, sat where Elsie's driveway lay now. And the house looked unoccupied. But so much seemed the same. Including the dusty turquoise shutters and . . . one missing. She flipped the photograph to the back side. "'Elsie and Heinrich Ackerman home, Christmas 1990. Forever grateful.'"

"Elsie Ackerman? Was she married more than once? Is Raymond her maiden name? This house. It's so similar, but different. Bizarre, isn't it?"

"Here's another view." Gabe handed her a black-and-white image this time. Scalloped corners bent with age.

"'Elsie and Heinrich. March 29, 1945. Near Freinsheim. May their soldier find his way home.'" Alexis struggled to find her breath. "It's the same house."

"Almost fifty years earlier. If I remember correctly, weren't parts of Germany liberated in March of 1945, when Allied Forces took over?"

"I'd have to look it up. Where did you find this?"

Gabe dug through the other small items in the metal box. "The color photo was nailed to a wall stud right here." He pointed to a spot close to where the sidewall and the floor met.

"An odd spot to post a picture." She lowered herself onto an overturned bucket. "Where'd you find the box?"

"I pulled up a floorboard, just to see how hard it was going to be to remove them intact. Easier than I thought. This was underneath it. So I had to pull up another board to get it out."

"Of course you did."

"There's some cool stuff in here. Discharge papers for Sebastian Brownell." Gabe held the paper toward the light. "According to the birth date, it would have made Sebastian ninety-three now."

"Gabe, this must belong to Elsie's father."

"Which Elsie? Ours? Or the one 'near Freinsheim'?"

"The Elsie in the photograph looks to be in her forties in 1944. She'd be long gone now."

"Right."

A draft brought on another full body shiver. "We can't paw through these things, Gabe. They don't belong to us."

"Aren't you curious?" He lifted the box as if tempting her to investigate.

"Curious about what?" Elsie's voice—their Elsie's—pierced the dust-moted, chilled air.

"DON'T BOTHER COMING UP, Elsie. We'll come down," Gabe called, sliding both pictures into the metal box and tucking it under an old tarp.

"Gabe," Alexis whispered. "What are you doing? We can't hide this."

"I have good reasons. Tell you later. Come on." He helped her to a standing position.

"No bother coming down," Elsie said. "I thought I should let you know I won't be here tomorrow."

"You're leaving again?" Alexis watched her steps as she descended, holding tight to the handrail. "You just got back."

"These things happen."

"What things?" Gabe asked.

Elsie stood at the foot of the stairs in her barn boots and work coat over baggy jeans. "I prefer not to talk about it." She turned to walk away. "Thought it wasn't fair if I didn't let you know. Especially since you'll probably want to keep an eye on Cat Astrophe."

"Elsie"—Alexis navigated the last couple of steps— "shouldn't we have some contact information? In case we need to reach you? For a decision or something?"

"You have my cell phone number."

"You don't keep your phone on. I've tried."

"Leave a message."

Gabe caught up to Elsie. "But what if you're in a horrible, nasty car crash and they can't identify the body and all they have is part of your address on your drivers' license and—"

Elsie stopped, turned, and addressed Alexis. "Now, right there is a man who will not give up. Such an endearing quality, isn't it?" She rolled her eyes and directed her next words to Gabe. "I told people Ms. Blake's number. If all else fails, the state patrol can call my sons." She mumbled something under her breath and unlatched the door to the chicken coop. "You two coming in with me? Or are we done here? Seems like there might be something to occupy your time in that shell of a house, if you've nothing better to do."

Dream client. Absolute dream client.

"Gabe, 'horrible, nasty car crash'?"

"Too much, do you think?" He leaned closer to get a shot of the empty papier-mâché crèche drying in late afternoon snowlight—a blue-pink light—on the kitchen window.

She was supposed to be the one in control. That was the arrangement. *Need to regain control. Because . . .*

Because she needed to find something she could control. She'd never been able to control anything as a child. Certainly not her career to date. She couldn't make anything perfect. It was beyond her. What made her think she could run with the big dogs, attempt something as outrageous as compete for a television slot most of the design world coveted? What made the producers pick her as a contestant? So they'd have her to mock? Had they planted Elsie? And Gabe? *This is going to be fun to watch. We'll wind up with more than enough footage for a blooper show.*

The hammering didn't help. With three crew members working at once to get the floor installed, the irregular rhythm of the pounding, the jarring sound of the pneumatic nail guns sounded more like war than progress.

War. The metal box under the floorboards in the hayloft. The date on the photo couldn't have been coincidence. Elsie's father wouldn't have been vacationing "near Freinsheim" around Christmas 1944. Maybe the photograph wasn't even his. Maybe it belonged to the people who'd owned the property before Elsie's father purchased it.

But Elsie said he'd often escape to the hayloft to be alone. He would have seen the color photo—the 1990 version— nailed to the wall in that section. Sebastian Brownell. Had Elsie mentioned her father's name or his surname?

Alexis forced her attention back to her laptop screen and the proposed menu for the Christmas dinner scenes. Photogenic food. Elsie would likely insist on making the meal. Alexis could make sure it was served on platters and in bowls that fit the new décor and set the scene.

Sebastian Brownell. The name interrupted her thoughts again. And the similarities of the two fieldstone farmhouses. One here, so close to the edge of Lake Michigan. The other in the heart of WWII Germany. They were connected. But how? And was that the story she'd been waiting for?

A story, a connector, a draw for why she was there, in a small town with no personal ties for her, with a woman who didn't appear to like her, and a task that grew more impossible by the hour. *The story of restoring.* That was why the script hadn't been coming together for her.

Could she weasel the ballad she needed out of Elsie? Not likely. But she might get a clue from Elsie's father, if his name was Sebastian Brownell.

And if it wasn't for the fact that his dementia was full-blown.

Shot down. Her idea was shot down before it could be implemented.

But that had to be the key. The Christmas she needed to portray in the video wasn't a dinner, an event, or even the unveiling of a home restored. It wasn't merely a man-made anniversary of a birth announcement. It was a whole story.

The pneumatic nailers grew nearer. She moved from the sofa to the kitchen island before the crew had to ask. The basement apartment Gabe had let her use called like a mega-screen advertisement for peace and quiet. He'd gone back outside, walking the property, capturing the snowfall at its most picturesque. She needed a story to accompany the beauty.

Elsie stood at the entrance to the kitchen, stocking-footed.

Can you open your heart enough to be a storyteller, Elsie? "Come on in. They're done with this section. The stools for the island overhang arrived about an hour ago. Let's unpack a couple of them so we have a real place to sit."

"How many did you order?"

"Four."

"It'll be just me most of the time. We might as well say all the time."

Alexis used a box cutter to slice through the packing tape on a massive carton the crew had pushed into the entry to get it out of their way.

"How are we going to do this between the two of us?"

"I'm learning to do a lot of things with one arm. And a hip. Or foot. It isn't"—she grunted—"graceful. But it gets the job done. Can you reach the other end to finish cutting? I'd like to spread the box as if we were . . . butterflying a chicken breast." Quick, a different example for the chicken woman. "Or a pork chop."

"I've never done either, but I assume you mean this." Elsie laid the box open so they could access the bar stools without having to slide them out.

"Exactly like that. I can handle this one. Can you get the other?"

"Sure. No assembly required?" Elsie looked the furniture over. "I kind of like these. They're different."

"See if you think they're comfortable enough for you and your guests."

Elsie tested the seat, back, and footrail and pronounced them comfortable enough. "But I don't have guests, like I said."

"You could use them when your children or grandchildren visit, Elsie."

She leaned against the island, arms crossed, and sighed through her nose. "I have two sons. And five grandchildren. Whom I never see. So you can return a couple of those stools and get your money back."

On an ordinary day, Elsie would have used that opportunity to slide off the bar stool and out of the room, leaving Alexis with a bevy of unanswered questions. But the woman hadn't moved.

"If you're expecting them to be here for that dinner at the end of this, they won't be," Elsie said. "I stopped asking a long time ago. They're not coming."

CHAPTER EIGHTEEN

WHEN RALPH WALKED INTO the kitchen to get a drink of water, Elsie said, "If the weather isn't too bad, you can have the men re-install that missing shutter."

Ralph looked to Alexis for confirmation. She mouthed "*No*" while Elsie's back was turned.

He shrugged an "*Okay*."

Addressing Alexis again, Elsie said, "I don't know why it was so important to me that the house have that flaw." Elsie rubbed her forehead. A two-inch scar near her hairline flushed pink then faded with the action. "Maybe you were making the house look too perfect. Life isn't perfect. I don't know why I insisted." She sat back, palms on her work-dusted thighs. "Maybe I'm the crazy old woman my sons think I am."

Elsie had been so resistant to touch, but Alexis reached out and grabbed one hand in hers. She held it for several moments while searching her brain's archives for a comforting response. When none showed up, even after she prayed, she stayed quiet and held on.

A few weeks ago, her task list or agenda would have taken

precedence over presence, over sitting with someone with a long-broken heart. Alexis wanted to ask her about those missing-in-action sons and grandchildren, about her father. Was his name Sebastian Brownell? And what did Elsie and Heinrich—a farm family in Germany—mean to him? Were they relatives?

But questions would have to wait. The two women sat together as the erratic, unmusical rhythm of the nail guns performed their duties at the other end of the open-concept room.

Open concept. *Please be open with me, Elsie. It might help to have someone to talk to, especially someone looking for the story line. And someone who cares, whether you know it or not.*

"I should pack," Elsie said. "Early start tomorrow, with it being—" She stopped herself.

"Do you need some help? We could talk . . . about the menu for the Christmas dinner. And about whom you would like to invite in place of . . . family."

"Did I say pack?" Elsie slid from the stool. "I meant nap. Don't have my quota in for the day yet."

The fading light reminded Alexis that they fast approached the shortest day of the year. Hours and hours and hours of darkness. Dark as the workday started. Dark when it was over. So much darkness. Right before the celebration of the One who came as the Light of the World. She'd never considered the irony before.

"The people walking in darkness have seen a great light."

Isaiah. Same chapter as the verse of promise, "Unto us a child is born." Same chapter. She'd read it that morning.

Elsie, we can put better light fixtures in your house. But we're not the light source you need.

"WHEN DID YOU do this?" Alexis watched the video snippet on Gabe's handheld camera while he drove them into Algoma.

"While you two were sitting at the island."

"I can see that."

"Don't worry. I had the sound muted, since neither of you were wearing mics anyway."

Alexis replayed the scene. It was one of the first they'd filmed that didn't make her cringe over her hair or posture or hand gestures (one-hand) or stage smile. The sling was hidden by the angle. But even that wouldn't have mattered. What she saw in the frame was compassion. More effective than makeup and soft lights.

"Did you get Elsie to talk?" Gabe asked.

"A little."

"About Sebastian?"

"We didn't get that far." Alexis turned off the camera. "I think we should take your dad something he really likes for supper. And maybe play a board game with him tonight."

"Rabbit trail."

"Same trail. I wonder if he'd like to do some research while he's still recuperating."

"To find that house near Freinsheim?"

Alexis tucked a stray hair into her man-bun. "It's near Mannheim. I looked it up online." She paused. "But no. Not that. To find Elsie's sons."

GABE MOVED HIS DAD'S HOT COCOA to the side and laid a series of photographs on the coffee table. "So, here's what we found in the hayloft."

"Gabe." Was he intent on sabotaging the progress Alexis was finally making with Elsie? "We agreed not to touch what was in that box."

"You agreed with yourself, Alexis. I never thought it was a good idea to ignore it. Besides, I didn't touch it. I used a stick to move it around so I could photograph the items. So, Dad, can you help us figure out—"

"I'm not comfortable with this."

"Me either, son."

"Thank you, George." An ally. "I think it's imperative that we focus our attention on finding Elsie's sons. It's possible we can talk them and their families into coming for Christmas. It doesn't matter what stood between them. It's Christmas. And with the possibility of our *Restoring Christmas* episode actually airing next year, don't you think they'd want to be part of it? Fifteen minutes of fame and all that?"

Gabe dropped another toasted marshmallow into his hot cocoa, careful to shield the splatter with his hand. "Or, the thought of a televised reunion might send them fleeing further."

"That's a possibility," George added. "Remember when we had to take that wedding video off our website because one of the bartenders was in witness protection?"

"I don't think Elsie's sons are criminals, George."

"On that cheery note," Gabe said, "could we get back to what we do know? Without coming straight out and asking her, or snooping in her room when she's gone—"

"Gabe!" Alexis choked on a Christmas cookie. One of George's friends kept him well supplied.

"I'm not advocating that. What I'm saying"—Gabe sighed—"is that we have no information to go on about her sons, without her cooperation. We know she moved to Algoma after her husband died. But she said *she* moved in here to take care of her father. She didn't say her boys—who would have been grown men by that time—came with her. So we won't have any local records to use. How many Raymonds do you think there are in the country? Did she ever say where they lived before she moved here?"

"No." Alexis picked another cookie from the assortment on the plate. Bad for the scale. Good for contemplating.

"Could we start with the clues we already have, then?" Gabe's eyes danced.

"We're not even sure this Sebastian Brownell is related to Elsie. He might be a previous owner of the property, or a collector who found these things in a box of junk at an estate sale in Nebraska." Why did her elbow pick now to flare up? Tension? Bah, humbug.

"That'd be easy to find out," George said. "You two probably have editing to do. Give me tomorrow. I'll see what I can come up with."

"Thanks, Dad."

"Now"—the older man adjusted his position in the recliner—"I suggest you two kiss and make up."

Gabe's thumb stroked a spot on his cheek, a spot with which she was all too familiar. "We're not . . . fighting. Are we, Alexis?"

"No. Difference of opinion."

"Agree to disagree, right?"

"Right." She kept the groan in her throat to herself. She was going to have to apologize for that kiss sooner rather than later.

She caught him thumbing that same spot on his cheek an hour later when they worked through the footage he'd shot that day. They sat at the small table in the basement apartment, but he kept missing the video cues.

"Gabe. We wanted to edit out—"

"Ahk. Sorry. Distracted."

Did she have to know how she felt about him before she could explain the thanks-for-being-on-this-journey-with-me spontaneous kiss? Talking about it might be the exact wrong thing. And an apology might make *him* think *she* thought it was a bigger deal than it was, which it wasn't. Not at all.

"Ugh." This time the groan escaped.

"What's wrong?"

Why, nothing. Nothing at all. No. That approach would never work. "It's the lighting."

Gabe leaned closer to the computer screen. "I was trying to make it look washed out like that, then as we zoom in on the front door, it gets crisper and crisper until we see the stark black latch against the— You're not even looking at the screen. Oh."

"What do you mean, 'Oh'?"

"You were talking about the lighting in the apartment." He swung around toward the living area and sighed. "You can turn the tree lights on if you want. It would brighten up the place."

"That's not what I was thinking." *At all.*

"It's not fair for you not to have a tree this year because I'm struggling with it."

She hadn't often heard Gabe Langley admit he struggled with anything. But the connection between his tree and his mom's death . . . Who wouldn't be affected by a grief touchpoint like that? "I'm not going to be the one to flip that switch, Gabe. I . . . I haven't even put up a tree for the last two years, so you're ahead of me on that score."

"Why not? Why would *you* not have put up a tree? A spectacular one, at that."

Had she inadvertently dishonored his revered tradition? His question sounded like she'd recommended removing the cream center from an Oreo. "Christmas and disappointments have gravitated toward one another in my life. I have a place of my own now. I chose not to get a tree. Besides, have you tried buying a Christmas tree from a lot in the heart of the city?"

"It's not like the movies?"

"Only the Christmas disaster movies."

He was still for almost a minute. "Well, just so you know, I don't mind if you want to have the tree lights on . . . if I'm not here."

"Not going to happen."

"It looks a lot better with the lights."

An ache rose within her. She ached for him and what it must be like to have made promises to his mother that she couldn't watch him keep. What it must be like. What it *was* like. *Opposite ends of the reasons spectrum, Gabe, but we aren't as different as I once thought.*

"I'm going to run upstairs and make sure Dad's okay. After I get him settled for the night, I'll be back. Feel free to scroll through these still shots and mark your favorites."

"Want me to make some popcorn?"

He hesitated. "Sure. If you want."

Gabe had been gone from the room ten minutes when the phone rang. Not Gabe's number. Elsie's.

"Elsie, it's so late." Alexis checked the time on the computer.

Later than even *she* thought. She'd offered Gabe popcorn. They hadn't even had supper.

"Did I wake you?" Elsie's voice sounded as cold as the night.

"No. No, it's not that. I'll be up for hours yet. I thought you were usually heading for bed by now."

"I was. Until I got a message that someone had called the long-term care unit, asking for Sebastian Brownell."

"Oh."

"The staff thought it was curious and thought I should know. Turns out, it was George Langley."

"Yes. Gabe's dad."

"Well." The word was more air than sound. "Don't bother showing up in the morning. You're all fired."

CHAPTER NINETEEN

"You can't fire us, Elsie."

"Why not?"

"The renovation is a gift. No financial investment on your part. My time, Gabe's time, Ralph and his team, the materials, they're all a gift. And you signed a contract."

Nothing. No response.

"Elsie? I didn't mean that to sound . . . "

"Ostentatious? Condescending? Threatening?"

Her throat too tight to speak, Alexis let the tears fall without bothering to wipe them. What defense did she have? That Elsie had been difficult? That she didn't communicate with them? That she was—

Broken?

"Elsie, I'm sorry."

"For meddling?"

"Among other things."

"What might have happened if you'd asked me if you could visit my father? Go along with me to see him? Did you think of that?"

"I assumed you'd say no."

A long silence. "Probably would have. At least the first time."

Alexis could visualize the slope of her shoulders, the crease in her brow.

"I didn't want all this fuss in the first place. You know that," Elsie said.

"But you also knew what was on the contract. You agreed to the terms."

"And now I'm un-agreeing. Wasn't there something in the contract that said, 'No messing with the home owner's private life'?"

I hope not. George is probably halfway to finding out where your sons live. And Gabe is likely booking flights to Germany to see that house for himself. "Elsie, could we sit down and talk? We need to talk it all out. I'll tell George not to call the care unit again." *Slow down, Alexis. She's already overwhelmed.* "But beyond that, we really need to talk in order to make this work."

"I don't want this to *work*, Alexis. I don't want us to talk. I don't want to get 'real and vulnerable' and spill my secrets so you can make a television show out of it."

Was that the idea she'd given? Did she have to admit it might have motivated her in the beginning? Things had changed. So much had changed. "I'm not looking for a show, Elsie. I want the story to shine. Your heart's story."

"What if I don't know what my heart's story is anymore?"

Believe me, I can understand that dilemma. "Would you let us help you find it?"

"Why would you do that? So you have a chance at the TV spot?"

"Because I care."

"Why on earth would you care about me?"

"Because you're irresistibly lovable?" Alexis prayed this was one of those times when humor could defuse a tense situation.

"That sounded like a line your Gabe would say," Elsie said.

"It did, didn't it? But he's not 'my' Gabe, just to clarify."

She huffed. "Is there anybody who isn't delusional these days?"

"Elsie . . . "

"I have to go. How did that ornery cat get in here? I haven't changed my mind, Alexis. You're a nice enough young lady, but we're done."

"Elsie, your house is a hollow shell right now."

"It was hollow before you got here."

ALEXIS TEXTED GABE. No response. George might have been in bed already, but she thought Gabe would have stayed up longer. She thought he was coming back.

What a disaster, on every level. Alexis was no counselor, but design clients weren't merely business contacts either. It cut deep that Alexis had been a disappointment, and that it had taken her so long to see past the needs of the house—past her own career needs—to the needs of the one who occupied it. Gabe had encouraged her to listen. She thought she had. But most of the time, it was for her own agenda.

Look where that had gotten them.

She texted Gabe again. Still nothing.

Two spots in the small apartment drew her when her mind numbed or thoughts whirled too fast for coherency. The wall of windows facing Lake Michigan, overlooking the shore-hugging town, and the unlit Christmas tree—sober, dark, but still beautiful in its hope potential. Tonight, the tree.

She'd lived with the tree long enough to have memorized the ornament placement. A videographer might be expected to include miniature camera equipment ornaments and tiny framed photos. Tucked among them were word ornaments—Courage, Hope, Endurance, Peace, Integrity, Honesty, Freedom, Fortitude, Fearless, Brave, Forgiven, Restored . . .

Alexis let her focus linger on the Restored ornament. She'd studied that tree since the end of October. Restored hadn't been there before today, had it? The word had been carved into the handle of a three-inch rustic hammer with a square-head nail almost the same size attached cross-wise to the back of the tool. The kind of nail they'd found when ripping up the underlayment of Elsie's home. A small wreath encircled it all.

It had to be new to the tree. She would have noticed the connection before now.

Gabe had given her permission to light the tree, if she wanted. She'd insisted it was his to light, when he was ready.

What would these words look like lit from within? What would a crude hammer and nail—*Restored*—look like with light shining around it?

And why couldn't she have seen the connection before it was too late?

They'd walked on . . . well . . . eggshells with Elsie from the beginning. She would not forgive them for this one.

It would have been funny if it wasn't so tragic, but the thought that circled back was that a person often feels the compulsion to pray at the very moment when they haven't got a prayer.

THE FINANCIAL SIDE of the disaster struck her shortly after midnight, like an out-of-control jackhammer. Not only would she lose the most important boost her career would ever know, but now all the costs incurred during the process so far—wages, materials, equipment, furniture, décor items she'd collected—fell on her shoulders. The profits she made from a design business few knew about would mean it would be a long time before she could dream, expand, or develop a workable marketing strategy. Double-punch.

And Gabe hadn't come back.

The bed lost its comfort factor. It too was borrowed. *Like the one the Christ Child needed.*

Now she was thinking like Gabe, everything tying back into Christmas somehow. She got out of bed and sat on the couch without turning on a light, the comforter wrapped around her.

The snow stayed cleaner than it did on the streets of Chicago. Moonlight on snow poured through the windows, making lamps unnecessary. It cast its light on the reflective ornaments on the tree. When the furnace kicked on, moving air stirred some of them. One of the word ornaments must have been in a good position to catch the current. It swiveled back and forth. *Peace*.

Here? Now? Asking a lot, isn't it, God?

She heard her words to Elsie. "You can't fire us. It's a gift."

Peace was a gift, too. God wasn't commanding her to *be* at peace. He was offering it as a gift.

When the furnace finished its cycle, the swivel motion stopped. Peace stilled.

With the project aborted—all of it—the other contestants now had a fifty-fifty chance at the *Restoring Christmas* special. Good for them. How could she do anything else but wish them well? She hadn't wanted to know their names, their challenges, their design histories. It helped keep Alexis from feeling in competition with them and focused her thoughts on producing an excellent product.

Now her attention would turn to packing up, saying good-bye to Algoma, saying good-bye to George, and—her *thought* tightened like her *throat* did when it hurt to say what she needed to say. Gabe. A conundrum. The most fun irritant she'd ever met. Facing every glitch with the kinds of words that hung on his Christmas tree, but holding tight to his grief and the shadowed stories that sobered him.

What might their relationship have become if it had time to develop?

For a moment, she thought about turning the thermostat higher so the furnace would have to kick on, have to stir the peace again so she could see it alive, not dormant.

What would Elsie do with her house in that state of "almost there"? Live with it that way until the day she died? It wasn't what she deserved.

The furnace fan reported for duty.

Peace danced in the moonlight.

Thanks for the gift, Jesus. I'll take it.

How had she managed to fall asleep on her bad arm? And what was that sound? The smell, she recognized. Morning breath. The sound? Her phone. Muffled by . . .

She found the phone under a couch pillow and stared at the screen until it came into focus. Gabe's number. And it was four in the morning.

"You just now got my text messages?"

"Alexis, I could use your help. I know it's early. Back-end-of-a-chicken early."

"What do you need?"

"Can you help me out? I'm at the police station. And I need a ride home."

She'd lost all her words again. *Say something. You have to say something.* "I'll be right there." *Have yourself a merry little Christmas, Alexis.*

She would have expected his speech to be slurred or his voice to hold at least a shade of remorse if he'd gotten into . . .

Alexis wouldn't let her mind go there. He'd been clean—free—"long enough to know it was possible." He'd said it himself. He'd also said, "and short enough to know not to let my guard down."

Gabe, of all nights . . . !

CHAPTER TWENTY

WHAT HAD HE DONE?

The question looped through her mind from the moment she heard his voice on the phone. Four in the morning. Police station. Not a good combo. He couldn't drive himself home. *Gabe, what have you done?*

Did she know him well enough to believe his personal rehabilitation had no chinks in its armor . . . or missing field-stone in its foundation?

She'd ridden with her aunt Sarah more than once when one of her parents—or both of them—had been released from jail or kicked out of rehab. Spewing promises. Already planning their next hit.

Love, Jesus, and years of counseling had brought her to a place where she could rehearse those memories without letting them cripple her. They hadn't changed. But she had. *But if that's as true as I claim, why does my heart feel as if it's limping?*

The police department, across the street from Tina Marie's Boutique on Fremont and half a block from their table at Caffé Tlazo—*limp*—and two blocks from the site of their boardwalk board meetings—*limp, limp*—wasn't busy at shortly after four in the morning. She parked behind Gabe's van.

Does he need me to bail him out? Do jails take credit cards? No. There's a simpler, though undoubtedly Gabe-dramatic explanation for why he called me. Has to be. God, please, there has to be.

Inside the building, Alexis found Gabe engaged in conversation with a uniformed officer and a fifteen- or sixteen-year-old young man with his hands deep into his pockets and shoulders hunched so high his ears were hidden. The officer took the boy by the arm and directed him away from their huddle toward a door at the end of the hall.

"Alexis. Thank you so much for coming." He wrote something on a clipboard at the desk. "I'm so sorry for getting you out of bed at this hour. Did your pumpkin . . . car start okay? It hasn't been run much."

"Gabe, what am I doing here? Larger question. What are you doing here?"

"Yeah. Sad story. But I thought we were done with *larger* questions." He slipped into his coat and led the way to the exit through which Alexis had just entered.

"No, no, no. Not done with the larger questions idea." It sickened her, but she couldn't help herself. She checked to see if his pupils were too wide. Couldn't get the right angle.

"I'll tell you on the way home, Alexis."

"You're leaving your van here?"

"Have to."

"About the *have to* part . . . "

"Dead battery," he said. "Wait. You thought—?"

"I don't understand any of this. And I don't want to judge. But—"

He stopped at her car door. He tapped the heel of his open palms on the roof, twice. Barely hard enough for her to hear the *thud* or see the emotion behind the action. "See? This is the hard part. When people you care about know your history, they make assumptions." He tried the handle. She'd locked it. Habit.

"Do you need me to drive?" he asked. "Is this too much for your elbow?"

It's not my elbow, Gabe. I'm limping. "I'm fine. So. You have a new goal now? *One day* clean and sober?"

It didn't take long to cross the empty predawn town, climb the hill, and pull into the driveway. But every minute of it held an awkward silence Alexis didn't know how to crack.

As he unbuckled his seat belt, Gabe said, "I thought you knew you could trust me." He got out of the car and walked a half dozen steps before returning. He opened the door but didn't get in. "You can trust me. I wasn't the one in trouble tonight. And it hurts more than I thought it would that you even wondered if I was. 'New goal?' Nice one. Way to twist the dagger, Miss Blake."

"Gabe . . . "

"I get it. I know it's part of the price I pay for decisions I made long ago. But I hoped—I really hoped *you* wouldn't doubt me. For . . . for a lot of reasons." He let himself into the house without waiting for her.

It was official now. She'd lost everything.

HER ALARM WENT OFF at seven. She wouldn't have needed it. She'd showered already by then.

Even though Gabe probably slept in, Alexis checked her phone way too frequently to see if he'd messaged her. Finally, at seven-thirty, she read, *Skipping Caffè Tlazo this morning?*

She texted her answer. *No.*

Had a spare battery in the garage. I'd appreciate a ride to my van.

Done. Half an hour?

Might need an hour.

We have to talk, Gabe.

Yeah. We do.

Hat day. She wasn't about to ask Gabe to put her hair up. He probably assumed they'd head to the work site after he got his van working. She should have come right out and told him they'd been fired so he could sleep as long as he wanted. But without question, they needed to talk.

She was ready and waiting in her car in fifty-eight minutes.

He exited the house in fifty-nine. She popped the trunk so he could load the new battery for transport to the vehicle that waited for it.

"I'm sorry I didn't reply to the texts you sent last evening. I . . . couldn't access my phone. What did you want?" His voice held none of its normal modulations. It lay flat. Lifeless. And it was her fault.

"We'll get to text messages." If the roads had been icy, she might have asked him to drive. Except for signaling to turn, she managed fine with her immobile arm's hand at six o'clock on the wheel and her right at two. Not standard procedure, but it worked.

"By the way," he said, his voice still missing its normal energy, "Dad and I are pretty sure there's a Sebastian Brownell at the Algoma Long-Term Care Unit. The staff member who answered the phone was all 'privacy act' with Dad when he called. So, we assume . . . "

"Yes, that's Elsie's father."

"How did you find out for sure?"

Alexis turned onto Water Street toward the downtown district. "Elsie. The center reported your dad's inquiry."

"Oh." He removed his wool cap and scrubbed his fingers through his hair. "What did she say?"

"The good news is that you'll have plenty of time for a nap later today. I won't have to look for expensive office space to lease on Michigan Avenue near WaterTower Place. And if that couple who begged you to do their Christmas wedding video hasn't found anyone else yet, you can still take that job. We've been fired."

"She gave us the pink slip?"

"Dusty turquoise. But, yes."

"Can she do that? Contractually?" Like a recovering pulse, the flatline of his voice started to blip a little.

Alexis had shattered someone's heart like others had shattered hers. She'd had no reason not to trust him—just a history that sent her mind straight to worse-case scenario. But that was no excuse. "Breakfast first or battery?"

"Which one has coffee?"

"All I needed to know."

Had his hurt mellowed at all since they parted? Could they get through this? If the tables were turned, would she have forgiven him?

Alexis ordered coconut oolong tea, craving the soothing fragrance as much as the small-but-mighty presence of the Asian cast-iron teapot it came in.

"Are you going to order something to eat, too?" Gabe asked.

"Do we have to?"

"We should eat."

She considered the menu, then told the staffer, "Carb something. Your choice."

The blond woman behind the counter took her hand. "Bad day, Alexis? I've survived cancer. Twice. I know just the thing. Trust me."

Alexis was known here. After just a few weeks, the staff knew her by name. *Algoma, I'm going to miss you. The church family. That stubborn red lighthouse. The curve of Crescent Beach.* "And put extra cheese on it," she said as she slid her tip into the jar.

Gabe stepped to the counter.

"Your usual?"

"Make it a double."

The blond woman smiled. "It's already a double. Triple shot?"

Alexis busied herself at the sweet-treats-to-go display and waited for Gabe to finish ordering. Then she picked a table as secluded as possible in a busy hometown café. The music overhead told her it was beginning to look like Christmas. She considered dashing off lyrics to a companion song—"But It's Beginning to Feel a Lot Like the End of the World."

"Hope isn't always shiny, is it?" Gabe took a chair at a right angle to her, on the right side, to leave her slinged arm plenty of room.

"You're thinking about *hope* right now?"

"Working my way up from utter desolation," he said.

She sighed. "You're further along on the journey than I am, then."

"I'll wait for you to catch up." He traced the stone pattern in the tabletop with one finger. "Now? Are you all the way to hope now?"

The tiny sobs that divided every inhale into three parts

were covered by coffeehouse noise. Weren't they? If she concentrated hard, she could keep the tears in storage, where they belonged.

"Alexis?"

"Ah, tea. Thank you." She watched the server carefully position the squatty cast-iron teapot on its warmer. Aromatherapy and thirst-quencher in the same drink. Gabe's coffee smelled as strong as it looked.

Gabe took a sip, winced, then set his mug aside. "Elsie canned us."

"You spent the night in jail."

His knee bounced. She pointed to the tea in her handleless cup and the pattern of the tiny waves on its surface. He slapped his hand onto his knee and subdued it. "Sorry. Old habit."

"In the jail, Gabe? I understand you weren't in trouble, but . . . "

"I do ride-alongs when there's a drug-related teen arrest. I'm an unofficial chaplain, I guess. It's part of what I do to give back after what I was spared."

She planted her good elbow on the table and rested her forehead on her palm. "Not what I assumed. I'm so sorry."

"I know. And I should have been more specific in my phone call. It didn't occur to me you'd—"

"My parents fell back into that scene so frequently."

Gabe's head jerked up and he sat back.

"But you're not them, Gabe. And I disrespected you for

no reason. I apologize. I admire what you're doing. It must be tough work."

"Your parents were . . . are . . . ?"

"Long, long, long story. Still waiting for their 'one day' goal."

"I'm free, Alexis. I'm cautious. And grateful. And way smarter than I was a few years ago. But back then, I never knew that—with everything else—I was risking the possibility of a relationship with someone like y— Ah, carbs," he said, acknowledging the server. "Thanks. That looks . . . filling."

Alexis needed to respond to him more than she needed food. But it did look and smell intoxicating. *No. Different word.* Divine. "Stuffed French toast?"

"Apparently."

"Real maple syrup?"

"Locally harvested."

"Gabe, would you pray over the meal for us?"

"Are you sure you want me to?" He thumbed that spot on his cheek again.

Now or never. Now or never, ever. "Gabe, I don't want this to be over."

He took her hand. "That's what I was thinking."

"JUST SO WE'RE CLEAR"—Alexis used her fork for emphasis— "by not wanting this to be over, you meant . . . ?"

"Exactly what you meant."

"Right. Which was . . . ?"

He glanced at her, then at the food on his plate. "The *Restoring Christmas* project."

Oh.

"Isn't that what you meant?" Gabe drank his coffee and looked at her over the rim of the mug.

She took another bite of cherry stuffed French toast. "Mmm-hmm."

"How are we going to win Elsie back?"

It's beginning to look a lot like the end of the . . . "I'm not sure that's possible, Gabe. You should have heard the pain in her voice. She's far more sensitive about her family life than we knew."

"But we're also closer than ever to helping resolve some of those issues. We know her maiden name. Brownell. That's a starting place. We can look up marriage license info for a Raymond-Brownell wedding between 1966, say, and 19—"

"Gabe. Snooping like that is what lost us our jobs."

"Well, we can't leave her house in the shape it's in now."

"We agree on that point."

Gabe scrunched his face and stared at the ceiling, as if reading his answer there. "She's gone for the next couple of days. Who knows why, but she is."

"Yes. But we aren't going to—"

"Ralph and his crew don't even know it's not business as usual. Correct?"

Now her good arm ached. And her knees. And her ankles.

Every joint, come to think of it. "We can't keep working if she told us we were done."

"You say that as if it's a bad thing."

"Gabe!"

"Hear me out." He shoved his plate aside and drew an imaginary rectangle on the table. "Here's the downstairs."

"Okay."

"This is pretty much finished. Bathroom and entry."

"True."

"The guys finished the kitchen floor and most of the living area yesterday." He circled that side of the rectangle.

"Except for the final sealer."

"Do you think they can get those base cabinets fixed today?"

Alexis shrugged. "I don't know."

"If I help?"

"The sealer takes how many hours to dry?"

"Okay, okay. What if we . . . what if we . . . ?"

"Gabe, it's impossible. We have to face it."

"Well, yeah. That's what makes it a challenge. And God-worthy."

She swirled a forkful of the breakfast delight through a puddle of syrup. "Do I want to ask what you mean by that?"

"There's Christmas for you again."

"Of course." She nodded her head, not necessarily in agreement.

"How easy would it have been for Jesus to have been born at the Nazareth Medical Center, wrapped in Macy's baby blankets, with family and friends waiting to hand out blue M&Ms, and Mary's greatest concern which infant photographer/videographer to use?"

"Nice reference to the importance of infant photographers or videographers."

"Thank you." His smile had returned. "With a few details changed, you can see how that would have been the 'doable' way for things to happen. But no. Too easy. Too humanly possible. What kind of splash would that make? And who gets the credit?"

"The doula?"

"Who?"

"Gabe, I know the Christmas story. Everybody knows the Christmas story."

"Yes, but the impossibilities! That's what makes it spectacular. Do you know how many detailed ancient prophecies came true because of the specific way, place, and lighting surrounding Jesus's birth?"

"You *would* notice the lighting." Alexis poured from the still-warm teapot. "You're looking for another Christmas miracle, huh? Isn't that getting a little cliché?"

"If we can finish up with the interior fixes and paint touch-ups today, and the guys can seal the floors right before they leave so they can dry overnight, can you do your thing with the doodad stuff tomorrow so the house is livable before Elsie gets back the next day?"

Doodads. "I have purchases yet to make. So little of Elsie's old furniture can be repurposed in the new setting. I thought I had a week to finish shopping. You told me about that architectural antique store in Door County. I wanted to make a trip there. And the Christmas décor? That's . . . it's impossible."

"Perfect. Let's go for it, then."

The flecks of gold in his eyes caught her attention. *I tried to let you give me a reason not to like you so much, Gabe. You're making it . . . impossible.* "Elsie may sue us for finishing after she told us we were fired. Or sue us for trespassing."

"We obviously won't be filming anymore. That's out of our control, sadly. But we have to give her something livable."

The moment of truth. "You're right."

Gabe glanced at his phone. "Ralph and the guys have started already. I'll head out there as soon as I get the battery installed. You take off for your sixty-second shopping spree."

"Only a slight exaggeration."

"And if you find anything sizable, give me a call and I'll bring the van. Is your arm going to be able to tolerate a day like this?"

"What arm?"

"That's the spirit."

CHAPTER TWENTY-ONE

SHE'D SPENT SO LITTLE TIME north of Algoma in Door County in the six weeks she'd been in the area. No wonder it drew the attention of tourists. This time of year, the cherry and apple orchards lay dormant, their limbs stripped of their rich fruit, but they still managed to form picturesque scenes with the tidy rows of trees that followed the line of the terrain.

She passed gift shops and specialty food stores she ached to visit, vistas she could only nod at, and photo ops that made her miss Gabe's presence beside her. *Focus, Alexis. Focus.*

So little of her original plan remained intact. As she drove, she recorded notes on her phone. What she yet needed for basics. What had shipped but lived in the storage shed. Even though Alexis was now footing the bill for the expenses, she couldn't do a halfhearted job, couldn't make Elsie's home less than what it and she deserved it to be.

When Alexis had told Elsie the project was a gift, she had no idea it would mean this.

She told her phone to remind her to call the Heart-and-Home producers and explain what had happened, that she was taking herself out of the competition. She couldn't tell them why without betraying Elsie's confidences and creating an even deeper chasm in their relationship. If Elsie wanted to give a full report, including Alexis's conduct, that was up to her.

She found a few pieces late in the morning and spent several hours in the architectural antique shops Gabe recommended. She could have filled a semi-trailer with purchases for future projects if she had any guarantee she'd still be in business after this, and if she wasn't now in the place she vowed she'd never be—paying out more than she was taking in.

Sunset threatened. The dining table and chairs she needed to complete the great room still eluded her. Farm table with the ability to expand when family came to visit. Alexis refused to give up hope for *that* Christmas miracle.

The trunk of her aunt's car held accent lamps, a narrow sofa table, items for the walls, a selection of antique books, and a box of vintage copper cookie cutters to go with the ones Gabe had found. If Elsie chose to decorate her tree this year, she'd have the option. Alexis wouldn't be around to see it, but Elsie would have the option.

"Finding what you were looking for?" the storekeeper asked. "We're closing in a few minutes."

"I suppose other shops will be, too?"

"This time of year, on a weekday? Most of them. The restaurants stay open later."

She'd forgotten to eat lunch. All those unique eating

establishments to choose from and she'd ignored them all. "I'm still searching for a particular kind of farm table. Haven't seen the one that—"

"That you can't live without?"

"It's for a client of mine." *Former client, but that would take me too long to explain.*

"How big?" The storekeeper headed toward the back of the long, narrow building. Alexis followed.

"Fully extended, I'd like it to seat ten. Or twelve."

The storekeeper kept moving, past the doorway, through an office that could qualify for hoarder status, and into a back area with no heat. "Got this in today," she said. "It comes with twelve chairs. None of them match in style, but they're all painted distressed white, like the table, with matching upholstery on the seats. Won't work for every person's taste. That's a pretty specific—"

"Dusty turquoise."

"Good description. I haven't put it on the showroom floor yet because I figured I'd have to re-cover the seats to make it more sellable. And it hasn't been cleaned up."

"I can do that."

"Oh, and one of the chairs is missing a leg."

Or a shutter? "That fits, too. How much?" Alexis's pulse raced.

"Make me an offer?"

She did. The storekeeper counteroffered. Alexis came up a little on her price. Done deal.

"The thing is, I need it tonight. Or early, early tomorrow. But I can't haul it in my pumpkin."

"Pardon me?"

"My . . . business partner"—*Close enough*—"is in Algoma. It would take him twenty-five minutes to a half hour to get here. Is there any way you could—?"

"Not tonight. Wish I could help. But my granddaughter's Christmas concert is this evening at the Gibraltar school. I have to get home, get some supper, get changed, drive up there . . . "

"I understand."

"And I'm sorry to tell you, but we're closed tomorrow."

What holiday was Alexis missing? A Scandinavian festival she hadn't heard about?

"It's our company Christmas party. I do all the cooking for it, and we have forty coming, so . . . "

Impossible. So that meant God had an idea when Alexis didn't. *Anytime, now.*

She chewed on her lip. "What if we dragged it out back and I brought my car around to . . . keep an eye on it . . . while I wait for my business partner and the van? Would that be okay with you?"

The storekeeper considered. "Do you have a concealed carry in that sling?"

"No. Broken elbow." Alexis opened her sling to reassure the woman she wasn't packing heat. *Good grief.*

"I can't turn on the security system until you and the table are gone or half of the Door County deputies will be called away from their supper tables. But I can do it remotely."

"You can? That would be great. I can call you when we leave the property?"

"I guess so. I'll get you one of my cards. And I'll take yours—the one with a magnetic strip I can swipe? Cash works, too."

Alexis handed the woman her credit card.

"Well, look at that."

"What?"

"My delivery crew drove in. Just in time to do the heavy lifting."

"Would they deliver to Algoma?"

"For a price. And as of two minutes ago, it's after hours, so they'd get overtime."

A too-small van. A too-long wait. Too short of a timeline. "Could they deliver early, early tomorrow morning?"

"Not before six."

In the *morning?* With all she had to do tomorrow, that might not be a bad idea. "Deal."

"GABE? I'M ON MY WAY BACK. I'll be there in—" Alexis clicked her seat belt and started the car.

"Wait. Don't."

"What?"

"Ralph's crew is finishing up the sealant for the floor. I found out where the cat was getting in. Through the dryer vent, of all things. Because we didn't have the dryer hooked up yet, all she had to do was nose her way through the tarp and there you go."

"Why can't I come home?" *Temporary home. Few more days. Minor detail.*

"Because I'm in Sturgeon Bay."

"Why?"

"To pick up a part. I kind of broke one of Ralph's power drills today. And to take you out to dinner."

That other minor little detail—meals. "That's sweet of you, but I'm done in."

"I'm here already."

"I can see the pout on your face over the phone, Gabe."

"It's a really nice place. Two words—seared scallops."

"I'm in." *How did he know that's all it would take?*

WHEN GABE STARTED their dinner conversation with, "We have to talk," the room dimmed. Or her vision faded. Or her blood sugar dropped to near-blindness stage. "*We have to talk*" hadn't ended well with them in the past.

"Ralph and his team didn't finish the base cabinets?"

"All done."

"Great. I can get in for staging tomorrow morning?"

"That's the plan."

She could see again. By candlelight, but she could see. "The frown lines aren't making me more comfortable, Gabe."

"My dad discovered a few things. About Elsie and her family."

Her mouth went dry. "He's not supposed to continue digging for information. Elsie will have a conniption if she finds out." *Oh, Gabe.*

"It's partly my fault. With last night's adventure and our rush today, I . . . in a manner of speaking . . . may have neglected to call off the hounds."

The most lovable irritant she'd ever met.

"But you're going to want to hear this. It explains a lot."

"You might as well tell me."

"You know how she never talks about her husband?"

"She's a widow. Grief affects people differently."

"Grief, I understand, Alexis."

"I'm sorry. Of course you do."

"I think it's another reason Dad took off on our research project with such enthusiasm. Tomorrow's the anniversary of Mom's passing. I think Dad appreciated something productive to do right now."

"Again, my deepest sympathies. It must be so hard on the two of you."

Gabe cleared his throat. "So it turns out Elsie's husband had been arrested multiple times for domestic violence."

"The scar near her hairline."

"She has a scar?"

"Her resistance to touch. Gabe, that's awful. Did he serve time? I mean, I know you can find out a lot of court information online these days."

"Unfortunately for some of us, yes, that's true. No, he didn't serve any time. From what Dad could gather, most if not all of the incidents stated 'wife refuses to move forward with charges.'"

"Do you think their boys knew? They had to know."

"This would have been twenty-five or thirty years ago. If she kept it from them somehow, they may have not understood why she acted differently than they expected when their father died. She took his life insurance money and moved to Algoma, to a farm, with chickens and a demented goat."

Tears stayed so close to the surface these days. Alexis had been strong, hardened some would say, so tears didn't normally come so easily. "All the more reason for us to make sure she knows she's cherished. Even if all we have is one more day to make a difference in her life."

Gabe's long pause told her his heart was heavy, too. "New décor won't do it."

"No. But our caring might. And the details we include that show we paid attention."

"Could go either way," Gabe said. "When she walks into that house day after tomorrow, she'll either be blessed, or she'll be so angry with us that she'll . . . "

"It's risky. Don't we have to try?"

Their meals arrived. Works of art. They ate in relative silence for a few minutes.

A thought niggled at the edges of her brain. Or maybe her soul. "Gabe, this *Restoring Christmas* concept means so much more than it did when I signed on."

"For me, too."

"Even with the show's potential gone—and I'm sorry about how that affects you and Langley Videography—I can't help but feel pulled deeper into its core. How many of us are walking around in need of that very thing?"

"Christmas?"

"A *restored* Christmas. Hope restored. Our past converted into something more suitable for how we live today."

"That one hits me in the gut."

"Painful memories retooled, like a scarred bowling alley turned into that beautiful work surface for the island. Good memories brought back home, like Elsie's father's couch bought back from the resale shop." The list was longer than Alexis realized when she'd started naming them off.

"Still waiting for your explanation of how Cat Astrophe fits into this idea."

The most lovable irritant. "Okay, mister. How about this? The flooring in Elsie's house was ordinary before the disaster. Nice, but ordinary. Now, it's that beautiful rich color and full of history, a connection to her father's hiding place. Every step she takes on that flooring will remind her of her relationship with her sweet father, even after he's gone." Gabe's optimism was rubbing off on her.

"You're sure he was sweet, Alexis?"

"Not sure. Hoping. I don't have any proof, but I think after her husband died, Elsie came here to find refuge."

"Her father must have done the same when he arrived at the place."

"Because it looked so much like the Ackerman house in Germany?"

"Dad discovered more intel. He should really become a private investigator. He's so good at it."

"What intel, Gabe?"

"Bits and pieces so far. But they might mean something."

"I'll spring for dessert if you get to the point."

CHAPTER TWENTY-TWO

ALEXIS USED HER LINEN NAPKIN to dab at the water she'd spilled during the earthquake of Gabe's announcement. "He did *what?*"

"Dad visited Sebastian at the long-term care unit."

"Gabe, this is unacceptable."

"It's okay. He went as one of the carolers from church. Blended right in. A group of volunteers from church sings carols at the care unit and the senior living centers during the holidays."

"Your dad was feeling up to that?"

"Said his back was killing him when he got home, but it was worth it."

"Cut from the same cloth, you two."

"Burlap? Linen? Silk?" Gabe smoothed his hand over his hair.

"Tell me what happened or it's no dessert for you."

"After they finished singing, the carolers mingled with the residents to wish them a merry Christmas and chat with them for a few minutes."

"And your dad sought out Sebastian."

"Wouldn't you?"

"From what Elsie says, he doesn't know her anymore. What kind of conversation could they have?"

"Enough. And you're right. He's a sweet old man. It's hard to do research with a man whose memories are gone. But he's brighter than the disease will let him show, Dad said. Disconnected from reality, but kind. Gentle. I can't imagine what that must have meant to Elsie the day she arrived at the fieldstone farmhouse and fell into her father's arms." Gabe swiped at his eyes with the backs of his hands.

Whatever resistance she still clutched melted. *This. This is the kind of man I could let into my life. Flawed, but grateful for his restoration. Serious when he needs to be, humorous most of the rest of the time. Bouncing back from disappointments with such agility. Rooted in God. Not afraid to grieve. Moved by others' pain.*

"Alexis?"

"Yes?"

"What do you think about that?"

"About . . . ?"

"About making it more permanent."

"Making *what* more permanent?" She risked taking another drink of her ice water, then switched to a sip of the tea.

Gabe's mouth and head tilted at opposite angles. "You checked out there for a minute, didn't you? We've been working full-on for weeks. Maybe we should get our desserts to go."

"Make *what* more permanent?"

"Don't worry about it. I'll take care of it."

Everything except her toenails ached. No. Toenails included. So many questions unanswered. Mysteries unsolved. Futures unknown.

She wasn't ready to give him an answer, whatever it was.

ALEXIS MOVED THE PILLOW that propped her arm in the night and threw it on the floor. Minutes later, she retrieved it and tried another position.

I should have pushed him to tell me what he meant. I might have still lost sleep, but at least I'd know why.

She rechecked her alarm to make sure it was set for 4:30. In the morning. *Yes. Good to go.* She couldn't miss the table delivery crew. Gabe told her he'd show up that early, too, but she'd insisted he wait until later. He'd missed enough sleep that week.

A sign of insanity? She was lying awake, worried about the sleep *he* was missing.

Alexis fumbled for her phone, clicked on her playlist for the "Still, Still, Still" song—the version with piano and cello—and set it to Repeat until further notice.

WHEN HER ALARM SOUNDED, she left the song on Repeat. This day promised to be everything but still. Maybe a soundtrack could gentle her through it and rein in her erratic thoughts. The schedule said, "Hurry." The word she preferred for a day like this was "intentional."

Despite the more-than-adequate soundproofing between the upstairs and the downstairs apartment, she moved through her morning routine as quietly as possible. She skipped the coffee grinder and opted for tea and a toasted bagel. She made a peanut butter sandwich for later. Protein. What else could she pack for the endurance test?

Nothing sat quite right in her stomach. Not the bagel or the tea or the thought of her clandestine decorating/staging operation. Not her assumptions about the kind of décor that would touch Elsie's heart. Or the flogging her self-worth might have to bear if Elsie called tomorrow to confront her.

Would it help if she left town before Elsie got back?

Chicken liver. That's what you are. Chicken liver. Face the music. Own it.

As if it were a devotional exercise, she made her way to the tree, with its silent messages shouting from its shadowed branches. *Courage. Fortitude. Endurance. Integrity* . . . It took all the fortitude she could muster not to flip the switch to turn on the tree lights. She fingered the wreath ornament with its rough hammer and nail. *Restored.*

Time to go prove that *Christmas* and *Restored* belonged on the same tree.

ALEXIS LEFT THE APARTMENT a half hour early for a ten-minute drive to the fieldstone house.

Gabe waited at the top of the stairs with a thermal carafe. "Let's ride together. It's symbolic on this last day."

"Wish Caffé Tlazo was open this early," she whispered. "Symbolically speaking. Not that we have time." The last word disappeared into the morning air.

Another quiet drive led them north of town along the shoreline to the side road that took them to Elsie's long drive-way. Predawn, its only illumination came from the van's headlights as it crossed the stone bridge and climbed the hill. The house stood strong and sturdy as ever, its trim's new paint and stronger porch saying, *"I'm not done living yet. Just watch me."*

Its missing shutter said, *"You don't know my whole story. You may never know my whole story."*

Gabe's broad shoulders rose and fell dramatically as he inserted the key into the back door. He carried the bulk of the new purchases inside while Alexis scooted ahead of him to look at the Abel-Bodied construction crew's finished product.

Nice work, guys. Except for its emptiness, the rooms looked ready for their new beginning. The men hadn't missed a thing. They'd removed all remnants they'd been there, including the dreary plastic draping. "They dusted?"

"That was me," Gabe said, depositing another package on the counter near the stove. "I thought it might help speed along the work you have to do today."

"Thoughtful of you. Thanks." The enormity of the task proved more stimulating than the coffee in the travel mug. "I'm eager to get started."

"What can we do before the delivery truck gets here? Never mind. That must be them now."

"I hope the table works in here the way I think it will. The extra leaves are stored inside the table itself, which is a help."

"I'll clear the back entry for easier access."

"I'll— Gabe. The mantel. You found the candleholders I wanted! You couldn't have made these, could you?"

He was out of earshot, no doubt opening the back door for the deliverymen. She checked the base of one of the candleholders. The initials *GL*—Gabe Langley—were burned into the bottom like a brand, along with a Scripture reference— 1 Peter 5:10. She'd have to look it up. The second of the three candleholders had the same initials, but a different reference— Acts 3:19–21. The third was different from the first two. That one she knew. Psalm 23:3—"He restores my soul."

Gabe, these are perfect. She rubbed her thumb over the *GL* impression, much as he had that spot on his cheek.

"Do that again," he said, sidling close to the fireplace with his handheld camera trained on her.

"Gabe, we're done filming."

"This is for . . . me. Please? The guys are kind of in a hurry to divest themselves of the monstrosi— Of the table."

She looked over her shoulder. Two smiling men held

opposite ends of the narrow but long table a few inches off the floor, waiting—apparently—for the all-clear signal.

Her face flushed. "Gabe."

"For me."

She complied. He would persist if she didn't comply. It wasn't hard to re-create the sense of wonder she'd felt at his thoughtful touches on the candleholders.

"And . . . cut!" he said, typical Gabe-style. "Okay, men. Bring her on in. Where do you want it, Alexis?"

It fit perfectly in the space between the kitchen island and the sitting area near the fireplace.

"You want us to move it an inch to the left?" one of the deliverymen asked. "They always want us to move it an inch to the left."

"Or the right," the other said.

Alexis shook her head. "No. It's exactly where it should be. Thank you." Would the entire day leave her breathless?

"We'll bring in the chairs then, get you to sign a couple of papers, and we'll be out of your hair."

Gabe left the men to that task and asked if Alexis knew what items she'd want brought in from the storage building.

"On our last full workday, I marked a few things with sticky-backed notes."

"Dusty turquoise?"

"Fluorescent pink."

"Way to shake things up." He took off and left her to

imagine the room finished. With these key anchor pieces in, it wouldn't be hard.

Midmorning had left its fingerprints on the windows before the table and chairs were wiped down and the area rug rolled out near the fireplace, side chairs placed, wall pieces hung.

"Where do you want this?" Gabe held a long piece of narrow, well-aged wood with divots carved in a row on top.

"On the island. It's an egg holder. I bought lemons to put in the depressions for now. Elsie can use it for her eggs if she wants."

"That look on your face is either utter confusion or it's telling me you need to be left alone for this stage."

"Is it weird that I need to be alone, but I want you near, and I need your help and advice, too? I need to think and putter."

"Brides and designers. So much in common."

"Is that the wedding videographer speaking?"

"I'll be outside. I have a little project I need to finish up."

"What kind of project, Gabe? Gabe?"

ALEXIS PRACTICED TRAFFIC FLOW, distance between each place to sit and a reading lamp and place to set a teacup or glass of water, comfort of the sofa with two pillows, three, no pillows. She settled on two. She checked the view from each of the side chairs and every position on the sofa. She sat at the kitchen island and turned to look out over the great room. She imagined sitting in one of the dining chairs closest to the skinny accent table behind the sofa and pronounced it spacious enough for a guest to get in and out comfortably.

All day, she'd watched the way the movement of the sun changed the light in the room as she worked. No awkward shadows.

The vignettes on the side tables and the kitchen counter needed no more tweaking. She hadn't decorated for Christmas as she'd hoped, but she did drape a garland of copper cookie cutters tied to a length of cotton rope on the mantel.

Only one spot still bothered her. *What is it you need?* The wall between two of the windows hadn't liked any of the options she'd tried there. A small shelf. A wall sconce. A wooden letter *E. No. Elsie wouldn't approve of that. R* for Raymond?

"Stymied?"

"Gabe. You're back. I wondered if you'd decided to head into town for real food."

"Getting hungry. Won't deny it. You were glaring at that spot on the wall as if had just said a bad word."

"It isn't saying anything. That's the problem. I don't know what it needs."

"Will this do?" From behind his back, he pulled two antique frames.

She would have swallowed her gum if she'd been chewing any. "The house in Germany."

"Both of them." He held the frames side by side, then one higher than the other.

"Gabe, what if Elsie . . . ?"

"She might know more than we think she does, Alexis. And even if she doesn't, they belong here, don't they?"

"Let me see that. What did you write on the paper on the back?"

Gabe tugged them away from her. She tugged back, one-handed. "Let me see them." Emotionally, the day was almost too much to bear. She sucked in a breath. "The verses you burned into the bottom of the candlesticks."

He took the frames from her hands. "The First Peter 5:10 verse says, 'The God of all grace . . . will himself restore, em-power, strengthen, and establish you.'"

I'll take that for me, if you don't mind. "And the other one?"

"Kind of my prayer for this house, no matter who's living in it. I mashed two or three versions together. Acts 3:20–21—'Then the Lord will provide a season of relief from the distress of this age, . . . that times of refreshing may come from the presence of the Lord . . . and he will send Jesus, whom he handpicked to be your Christ, whom heaven must receive until the time for restoring all the things about which God spoke.' So. I hope it's okay with you."

"Do you have a hammer and a couple of nails?"

Gabe handed her the frames again and pulled the hammer from his back pocket and retrieved two nails from his shirt pocket. "May I?"

She held the frames to the wall, then scratched two spots in the whitewashed, reclaimed wood.

After the photos were hung, she stepped back to see them in relation to the rest of the room. "I hope Elsie can somehow have a restoring Christmas, Gabe."

"I think that's what it's for."

CHAPTER TWENTY-THREE

"Is that the last of it? Alexis?"

This was not her design. Warmth spread through her as she surveyed the home's interior for the final time. It was God's design. Much better. And much harder to leave. "Did you take some final pictures, Gabe?" *For me.*

"I did."

She picked up the tiny, matchbox-sized remote from the mantel and clicked off the flameless flickering candles. On her way past the sofa, she plumped the pillows one last time. She straightened the Christmas arrangement on the dining table—fresh greens with touches of copper and teal. In the kitchen, she used a kitchen towel to clean a spot of water from the faucet arching over the farm sink.

"It's perfect, Alexis." He took the towel from her and draped it as she'd had it on the counter. Then he took her shoulders in his hands. "She'll love it. Good work." He bent and kissed her cheek. "There. We're even now."

She raised up on tiptoe and kissed him on the mouth.

"And now we're not. Even, that is." Heart-pounding, she lowered to flat-footed, but didn't lose his gaze. The music she'd played throughout the day—"Still, Still, Still"—played on. An entire verse. Neither moved. "Please tell me that wasn't a mistake."

"A mistake? That's what you call this?"

Heart completely out of rhythm. "Elsie!"

"What are you two doing in my house? What have you done? What have you *done?* Do you have no respect at all for my wishes?"

The way they'd turned, Alexis almost leaned back against Gabe's chest to escape the vitriol Elsie hurled. When Elsie walked deeper into the room, Alexis whispered to him, "Don't you get any farther away from me than this until the dust has settled, okay?"

"You really think the dust is going to settle yet this century?"

Alexis tightened her stomach. Or it tightened without her intentional effort. Every nerve ending sounded an alarm. They should have been long gone. Elsie said she'd be out of town for two days. No fair. This was one and a half.

No amount of defensiveness would justify the fact that they'd disobeyed her direct command—that they "cease and desist." They'd plowed ahead against her express wishes. But couldn't she be at least a little grateful that her home was livable?

Alexis should have known better. She stifled a cough. *How many times can I completely destroy things?* One would think *completely* meant the end of opportunity for ruination, but no. She kept finding ways.

Elsie seemed to take in every detail, touching everything, her jaw jutted so far forward, Alexis wondered if the woman would sue them for orthodontic repairs, too. Elsie fingered the copper pieces in the swag on the fireplace, the newly refurbished mantel, the rounded backs of the side chairs, the edge of the farm table.

When she stepped in front of the framed photographs of Elsie and Heinrich's house in the German countryside, her shoulders sagged.

Gabe tensed, as if ready to explain. Alexis lifted her hand to stop him. "Wait," she whispered. "Give her time."

Elsie grabbed onto a dining chair and lowered herself to her knees on the floor. She pressed the heels of her hands into her forehead and rocked forward and back. All Alexis could compare it to was video footage she'd seen of women at the Wailing Wall in Jerusalem.

Muffled sobs poured from the woman now.

Gabe grabbed Alexis around the waist.

"What are you doing?"

"I have to go to her. I have to. But I was ordered not to leave you, so you'd better come with me."

"I can . . . (hic) . . . hear you . . . (hic) . . . two," Elsie said between sobs.

They were at her side in less than a moment. Kneeling on the floor with her half a moment later.

"Where . . . where did you find these?" She lifted her face to the photographs.

Alexis nudged Gabe with her shoulder.

"I found them in the hayloft. Where your father used to go when—"

Elsie glanced his way. "You don't have to explain what a hayloft is, or that my father used it as his man cave."

"Man cave?" Alexis mouthed Elsie's words again to Gabe. He shrugged.

"I haven't seen these in years," Elsie said. "I wondered what he'd done with them."

"Did you go with your father when he took the photo from 1990, Elsie?"

"Yes. I'm the one who took the picture. Shortly after the fall of the Berlin Wall." She said nothing more.

"Can you tell us why that house meant so much to him?" Alexis asked.

She pinched her eyes shut. "Not now."

"Okay, Elsie. It's okay."

"No, it's not. I have a cramp in my leg. Help me up."

They helped her to standing, Alexis doing more guiding than lifting, and settled her into one of the side chairs near the fireplace. Gabe and Alexis sat together on the couch.

Elsie rubbed her calf and rotated her ankle, grumbling under her breath. "I knew I should have stopped to hydrate.

Why I had to be in such an all-fire hurry to get back here, we'll never— Well, I guess we do know now, don't we?" The last question flew straight to the two couch-sitters.

"Elsie," Alexis began, drawing two extra breaths she hoped were injected with courage, "we . . . I . . . we couldn't imagine leaving your home in such a state. We understood that you were canceling the show, canceling us and our involvement. But we had to make it livable for you."

"You didn't have to." She shifted in her chair. "If I were you, I would have poured tar down the drains and let the chickens have their way in here while I was gone. I imagine the cat tried."

"Good news on that front," Gabe said. "I found where the varmint— Where your cat was getting in. All taken care of. It won't happen again."

Elsie directed her attention to Alexis. "Is that boy always this chipper?"

Alexis patted his knee. "Pretty much all the time."

"Must be exhausting." She shook her head. "Let me say what I need to say."

"Yes, ma'am."

"I . . . was wrong. It's been a long time since someone . . . cared about me. And I thought all this you were doing"— she waved her hand toward the corners of the room—"was more for you than for me. Like I was—this house was—your project, a rung you could use to push yourself higher in your career."

So that's what it feels like when a lung collapses. Alexis pressed her slinged arm into her rib cage, as if that would help. "You're not . . . entirely wrong, Elsie. That served as too much of my motivation in the beginning. The words taste awful saying them right now. But they're true." She swallowed hard. Gabe slipped his arm around her. "My heart changed over time. I hope you can see that."

"I should have noticed it before I did. You tried showing me. I wasn't ready to believe it."

"Elsie," Gabe said, "are these photographs at all related to why you're estranged from your sons?"

She stared into the unlit fireplace. "I suppose in a way, they are."

"You can trust us with your story," he said.

Elsie opened her mouth, then hesitated. "I like those candle things on the mantel."

"Gabe made them for you."

"Elsie—the other one—the one in the picture—and her husband took my father in when he was shot down in an Allied air assault west of Mannheim shortly before Christmas 1944."

"I can't imagine how frightening that must have been." Alexis leaned forward.

"He walked for miles, bleeding, almost delirious, he said. Somehow, he stumbled into the barn on the Ackerman farm and pulled himself into the hayloft to hide. Heinrich found him there, unconscious but still alive, when he noticed the hay he forked down for his animals had blood on it."

Gabe rubbed his hand on his bicep. "He and Elsie could have been killed if they were discovered harboring the enemy." He looked at Alexis. "I watch a lot of the History Channel on weekends."

"They knew the danger. But they brought him into the house, cleaned him up, bandaged his wounds, and burned his uniform so they and he wouldn't be found out. They kept him hidden almost three months until that area was liberated. He spent Christmas 1944 with people whose language he didn't know, supposedly his enemies. Thousands of miles from home. But as safe as one can be during a war."

Alexis took Elsie's hand. She had to reach across her body to do it, positioned as she was with her sling in the way.

"Did your father stay in touch with them after the war?"

"They moved shortly after. Their son served on the opposite side. When my father could get help from an interpreter so they could correspond, they told him they cared for him the way they hoped another family would care for their son if he were injured. But soon after the war they were forced to give up the farm. He lost contact." Elsie sighed. "Those were the days before Internet, you know. It wasn't as easy to find someone as it is today."

"But he remembered that house. Including the missing shutter on the front." Gabe sat against the back of the sofa. "How did he wind up here?"

"And were you named for the woman who took care of him?"

"One question at a time." She stood. "Yes, when I was born about a year after Dad returned to the States, he and Mom chose the name Elsie on purpose. And he wound up here"—she nodded toward Gabe—"because he saw this house in a real estate ad not long after my mother died. That's all it took. I purchased it for him—which is what distanced me from my sons, who thought I was throwing away their inheritance. 'Mother, chickens? An outhouse? Have you lost your mind?'"

Alexis cringed.

"Now, if you'll excuse me, I have to feed those chickens. Gabe, you lay a fire."

He grabbed the remote for the fireplace and pushed a button. It sprang to life. "Done."

Elsie chuckled. "Okay, then. Alexis, would you put on the kettle for tea? You have a remote for that?"

"No. I'll have to do it the old-fashioned way." Tension left her body as if someone had pulled the plug on an inflatable pool. "I'd be happy to make tea."

"I brought home a pizza, not knowing what I'd find here. Do you think we can split that three ways? I suspect you aren't leaving until you've heard the rest of the story."

Alexis lit the candles scattered throughout on her way to the kitchen end of the room. She could only imagine what the house looked like from the outside with the light sneaking out the windows to sled down the slope of snow. *Thank You, God. Thank You, God. Thank You, God.*

She'd slapped the music off as soon as Elsie arrived home.

231

Now she tapped it on again. "Still, Still, Still." It fit better than it ever had.

Gabe retrieved Sebastian's metal box from the van. He'd intended to return it to the hayloft hiding place before he and Alexis made their final exit, he said. He hadn't gotten that far before Elsie's return changed their plans.

While the tea water heated, he helped Elsie unload her car, including the pizza box, which she'd wrapped in a fleece blanket to keep warm.

As Gabe folded the blanket, he whispered to Alexis, "You know, if she wants to put this blanket over the sofa, you'll have to let her."

It's her home, Alexis. Not yours. "I'll behave. I won't even flinch."

"And another thing," he said, pulling her nose-to-nose close, as they'd been when Elsie found them. "You wanted me to let you know." He drew a slow breath. "It wasn't a mistake."

CHAPTER TWENTY-FOUR

"So, THERE WILL BE EIGHT OF US for the Christmas dinner," Elsie announced when the last of the pizza was a faint, garlicky memory.

Alexis grabbed the edge of the island and held on. "What? You don't have to feel obligated to follow through with that anymore."

"What if I have a reason for wanting to go through with it?"

"I suppose it could be done." *Seems impossible at this late date, so it must be right.* "Do you want my involvement? It's your dinner."

"In a few minor ways," Elsie said. "Decorations. We need a tree. Can't not have a tree. And the food. There's the food. I'll be gone for a day or two right beforehand, so—"

"Elsie," Gabe said. "Burning question."

"They're all burning questions for you, aren't they?"

Alexis piped up. "No. Sometimes they're the *larger* questions."

Gabe dropped their plates into the dishwasher slots designed for them. "This one's bigger than big. Where do you go when you stay away for days at a time?"

"Considering our guests for Christmas dinner, I should 'fess up."

The expression on Gabe's face so closely matched what Alexis assumed hers looked like that she almost burst out laughing.

"I go to funerals."

Alexis and Gabe offered a collective, "Oh."

"Mostly for servicemen and women who are homeless, or who are in a VA home and die without family or friends. If I can help it, no military person's funeral will have nobody show up. Sometimes it's just me."

"How do you hear about all these funerals?" Gabe asked.

"I have connections with the VA and most of the VFW units from here to the Mississippi on one side and the Pennsylvania state line on the other. A couple of charitable organizations that serve the homeless. They know me."

"That's remarkable, Elsie. What a gift you're giving them." Alexis retraced their conversation to its genesis. "So, who's coming for Christmas dinner?"

"Hadn't I mentioned that? Some homeless vets I've gotten to know. How many can that table seat?"

"Ten," Gabe said before Alexis could answer. He had the strangest look in his eyes when he turned to her for confirmation.

"Actually, with all the leaves in"—she caught the subtle shake of Gabe's head—"ten is a good number."

Gabe exhaled. "Yes. About ten."

"Well, that's just right, then," Elsie said. "The three of us and my five guests. Room to spare. You can have everything ready when I get back, Alexis? I have to go pick them up in Milwaukee and I hate to make that trip all in one day, at my age."

"I'll . . . I'll do my best." She hadn't taken her eyes off Gabe, who still squirmed like he was sitting on a— *Oh, no. A secret.*

ALEXIS GOT HER WISH. As she and Gabe turned onto the side road at the bottom of the driveway, she looked back and saw Elsie's house—the fieldstone house—Hope House—lit from within. "Can we stop and get a picture of that, Gabe?"

"The lights, you mean? I already did. I snuck out when you and Elsie were standing in the kitchen together. It's harder to find excuses to sneak out now that Elsie has indoor plumbing, if you know what I mean."

Alexis waited thirty more seconds. "Ten, Gabe? You know that table can seat twelve when fully extended. Of course, we haven't had time to fix that one chair leg yet."

"We . . . may have . . . another couple of guests that night."

"Who? You have to tell me." She gave him her best insistent look, but he wouldn't be able to see it in the darkness.

"I promise I will. I need to do a little more investigating."

"Gabe, you know that only leads to people losing their careers"—she pointed at herself—"and all sorts of other problems."

"We're going to have a video to submit. I guarantee it."

"We lost how many days of taping? All the interesting part of getting the new floor in and the reveal. That's im—"

"You were going to use the word *impossible*, weren't you?"

"Maybe. Or maybe I was going to say impudent. Impersonal. Impish. Pick one."

His laughter filled the van. "Is it a mistake if I tell you I think I could love you forever?"

She let the question hang in the air longer than necessary. He deserved it. "Yes, it's a mistake."

"Ah. I see."

"You left in the word *think*."

ALEXIS HAD COLLECTED more than enough Christmas decorations she'd recently thought she wouldn't have an opportunity to use. The decorating wouldn't be her "larger question." As she added lights, with Elsie's help, to the five-foot cedar tree Gabe had cut from the edge of the property, she mentally worked and reworked the menu. Her cooking skills were adequate, but this meal called for something beyond adequate.

In a flash of inspiration, she dug out the business card of

the woman from whom she'd purchased the table. The storekeeper had mentioned cooking for their company Christmas party. Alexis called.

"Well, I'm glad the table is working out like you'd hoped."

"It is. In fact, my client is hosting a dinner on Christmas Eve for eight or ten-ish people. I'm calling to ask a favor. She's invited some homeless veterans to the table, and . . . "

"Is that for Elsie Raymond? God bless her. Is she your client?"

"You know her?"

"My husband is acting chaplain of the VA hospital. We know her well. What a gift she is. What does Elsie need? Donations?"

"You wouldn't happen to do any catering on the side, would you?"

"For Elsie? Happily. Tell you what. You have my email address there. Send me the menu. I'll take care of it. I have family coming for Christmas Eve, but if you could have someone pick it up at my place that afternoon . . . ?"

"I know just the guy. This is an amazing blessing. Thank you."

"Elsie's an amazing gift. It's an honor to help you do what you're doing. Can you send the menu yet today? I have some heavy-duty grocery shopping to do."

"I'll get it to you within the hour." She didn't dare ask the woman if her food was photogenic.

REALITY STRUCK ON December twenty-third. Elsie's house couldn't have been more beautiful. Alexis was free of her sling. Gabe had gotten the additional footage he needed and spent most of the day editing. Even though her arm was stiff and weak from lack of use, Alexis added finishing touches to the Christmas decorations, watched over Gabe's shoulder, and snuck away for some research of her own.

Elsie had left for Milwaukee early in the day to allow herself plenty of time to get there before dark.

As Alexis and Gabe finished up at Elsie's house and made their way back into Algoma, the familiar *farewell* feeling struck hard. They'd been given a few more days on the project. But it was so near its end. Even if they managed to pull off a reasonably successful video montage, good-byes were inevitable.

"Gabe, I thought of something."

"What is it?"

"Where are the homeless vets going to spend the night? Elsie can't put them all up in motels with Bayside, Seaside, Bayview, or Shoreview in their names, can she?"

"She'd made arrangements with a shelter in Green Bay, but I volunteered our men's group from church to get involved, and what do you know? Turns out there's more than enough room in the inn."

"Oh. Good. Good."

"What's on your mind now?"

"Going home."

"Yeah. We have a big day tomorrow. It'll be good to kick

my shoes off. And you probably want to put ice or heat on your elbow, don't you?"

"Not home to your apartment, Gabe. I'm thinking about a few days from now, when we're done editing and I have to leave here."

Gabe adjusted his hat. "Oh, that. I can stretch out the editing for months if I go slow enough."

"The submission is due no later than December thirtieth."

"Of *this* year?"

"Nice try. Yes, this year."

He drove in silence for another mile. "Do you mind if Dad and I come downstairs tonight for a while?"

"Sure. It's your place, Gabe. I'm the trespasser."

"I'll call or text you when we're ready and see if it's a good time for you."

"Okay. You won't tell me what it's about?"

"Half of the secret research. I think you need to know about it before tomorrow."

"Will it make me say, 'Gabe Langley!'?"

"Probably."

She expelled a week's worth of sighs. "Bring it on."

ALEXIS HEATED APPLE CIDER on the stove and stirred in two cinnamon sticks. She'd purchased expertly decorated Christmas cookies at the bakery. She'd intended to contribute them to the after-dinner conversation time tomorrow night, but she pulled out a few and set them on a small red plate on the coffee table.

The fire was lit. Counters clean. The smell of apple cider and cinnamon chased away the smell of the tuna melt she'd had for supper. She was ready. Maybe not emotionally. It was, after all, Gabe and his father.

Gabe texted a little before seven. They were in her/his apartment at five minutes after.

"Good to see you, George. How's your back?"

He crossed his arms. "I've been cleared to return to work after the holidays."

"That's great."

"One would think. Are these for us?" He grabbed a cookie before she'd finished forming the *Y* on "Yes."

"First things first," Gabe said. He stood behind the chair his dad had chosen. "I've needed to do this for a long time." He didn't walk toward Alexis but away from her. He flipped the switch for the tree lights. "Thank You, God, for giving me a great mom, for letting us enjoy what it was like to be loved by her, even though it was—if You don't mind my saying— too short. Thank You for the light she was to us."

"Amen."

Alexis could see the tree lights reflected in Gabe's eyes. "I wish I'd known her."

"She would have loved you," George said.

The three of them sat a long time in the fresh light of the newly awakened tree. Alexis turned off the table lamps and reading lamp so the light sources were reduced to the fire in the fireplace and the tree.

"'From the fullness of his grace we have all received one blessing after another,'" George said.

"We have," Gabe added. "Like this one." He pulled a folded paper from his pocket and handed it to Alexis.

She had to turn on a table lamp to see it clearly. A photograph of a man in his late sixties, early seventies. "Who is that?"

"That is Guest Number Nine for Christmas dinner."

"Should I know him?"

"Henry. Elsie and Heinrich's grandson, born to Heinrich Jr., who served on the opposite side of Sebastian in the war."

"We found him!" George celebrated with another cookie.

"Wait. He's coming to the dinner? Where does he live?" Alexis took another look at the photograph.

"Boca Raton."

"Florida? How—? When did—? He agreed to come?"

"Elsie doesn't know," Gabe said. "She will be floored."

"What does he do in Boca Raton?"

"Retired now, but he taught history for years. Can you imagine how excited he was at the prospect of meeting Elsie, the woman named after his grandmother?"

"So, he's coming."

George picked up the red plate. "Have a cookie, Alexis. Your blood sugar must be low."

"I can't believe this."

"He and his wife and one of their sons and family are staying in Sturgeon Bay tonight. I talked to them a few minutes ago. We thought we'd bring in Henry alone for the dinner. Then maybe on Christmas Day, Elsie would like to host their whole family for brunch or something. You know, farm-fresh eggs and cherry strudel."

"And you're not giving Elsie a heads-up to prepare for that at all, of course."

"Yeah, that's what I said, too, Alexis." George took a swig of his cider. "I made him run up to the Door and get some from one of the cherry markets. All but one of the strudels are still in our freezer."

She didn't want to ask. Couldn't ask what happened to the other one. Or about the other half of the Langley men's surprise.

CHAPTER TWENTY-FIVE

ELSIE CALLED AT THREE O'CLOCK. They'd stopped for gas in Manitowoc and would reach the house in a little over an hour. She'd opted for Route 42 along the lake, since the roads were clear, the sun shining, and the men—she reasoned—hadn't seen enough pretty scenery in their lifetimes.

Alexis stopped fussing with the place settings and made a note of one more thank-you card to write—the man from Gabe's church who had volunteered his seven-passenger van, and volunteered to drive it for Elsie. On Christmas Eve. The church lived what it preached. Okay, a thank-you note for the church, too, plus the members of the men's ministry who were housing the vets for the night.

No room in the inn? "Turns out there's more than enough room in the inn," Gabe had said. She'd never tire of his slant on life. Not a thought she could afford to entertain on a day like today.

He'd arrive with the food any minute. That would give Alexis time to figure out platters and serving spoons and—

The imprinted sound of hammering and power tools? Not a memory. Real time. She looked out the front window. Ralph's crew had returned with what looked like a pre-assembled ramp, the kind needed for wheelchair access. It hadn't occurred to Alexis that some of the homeless veterans Elsie invited might need wheelchair access. Some might be amputees. She should have thought of that. How did Ralph know? The usual suspect, no doubt. Gabe.

She stuck her head out the front door to greet the crew. "Thanks for giving up part of your Christmas Eve for this, guys."

"Our pleasure," Ralph answered for them all and added, "We'll sweep the snow off the porch here, too, when we're done. And the sawdust. You won't even know we've been here."

The goose bumps weren't from the cold. Love and kindness in action—in abundance—kept her in a state of awe.

The sight of Gabe's van pulling into the driveway and across the snow-hemmed creek ramped her heart rate. *Some* of that reaction might have had to do with her responsibilities with the food he was bringing. She stirred the mulled cider in the slow-cooker on the counter near the sink and cleared the surfaces to make room for the food.

Minutes later, she heard a muffled *thud-thud-thud* at the back door and a "Merry Christmas, but I could use some help here!"

"Merry Christmas to you, too, Mr. Langley . . . Come

on in." As she swung the door wide, the tension of wanting everything "right" dissipated. *Mist. Vapor. Gone.* Gabe stood with a stack of containers from waist to chin in his arms, the handles of plastic bags gripped in both hands, and an irresistible grin on his face.

"May I introduce you to Mr. Henry Ackerman." Gabe stepped aside. "Henry, this is the Alexis Blake I've been telling you about. Alexis, this is our Henry, grandson of Heinrich and Elsie Ackerman."

Henry stepped forward, a cane supporting each step. "Don't mind this," he said. "My artificial knee is getting used to me. A very blessed Christmas to you, Alexis." In his opposite arm, he cradled a large rectangular package wrapped with Christmas paper.

"May I take that for you, Henry?"

"I'd be grateful."

"Excuse me?" Gabe said. "I have burdens too."

"You're on your own, buddy. Let me help you over the threshold, Henry." She took the package and Henry's arm. "I'll be right back, Gabe."

"You help him," Henry said. "I'm fine. I'll take it slow."

"I don't think I can let go of anything, Alexis." Gabe wiggled through the doorway. "Just don't let me trip or bump into anything."

She guided him like backing a big truck into a tight parking spot.

He set the containers and bags on the island. "First load."

"Of how many?" Alexis calculated where she would put everything without destroying the peaceful ambiance she'd worked so hard to create. *Food chaos. We've moved from construction chaos to food chaos. People chaos is next.*

"Two more trips should do it. Your caterer pulled out all the stops. You should smell the van." He stopped halfway through the back hallway. "Alexis?"

"Yes?"

"Nice touch with the wreath on the back door. I have to tell you, I got a little teary-eyed when I saw it."

"I put one on the front door, too. I hope you don't mind my copying the idea from the hammer-and-nail wreath ornament on your tree."

"Genius."

"I'm glad you think so. I used a photo of it for the placards for the table settings. Restored seemed like a good theme for this gathering."

He laid his palm on the side of her face.

"Your hand is as cold as an ice cube."

"Do you mind? Your cheek is as warm as a . . . " He kissed the opposite cheek. "Testing for temperature."

He left her in the hall. She allowed herself ten seconds of wonder before she returned to the kitchen and their— Elsie's—first guest, the one Elsie didn't know could connect the dots of her memories.

IF AN ENLARGED HEART could be a healthy thing, that's how Alexis would describe this sensation. She listened to the harpist and cellist laying a soothing foundation to the evening, despite their awkward positions—the harp on the landing leading upstairs, the cellist several steps higher. "No room in the inn" in this case meant a tight squeeze but every heart in the home full to overflowing.

All were seated around the long, storied table except Gabe and Alexis, who prepared to serve.

"Should we start?" Elsie asked. "We're all here." She'd long ago dried the tears that fell when she met Henry and heard his parents' and grandparents' side of the story. New tears appeared now.

Another car pulled up the drive. Gabe skirted the table and grabbed the package Henry brought with him. "Back in a minute," he said. "Carry on." He tore off through the kitchen and out the back door.

Elsie's confusion registered clearly on her face. But conversation around the table soon diffused it.

Alexis side-stepped to the front window. *Oh. My heart.* If she didn't get away from this Gabe Langley character, her sinuses might never clear. She pulled the chair at the foot— or the head—of the table—the spot nearest the door—out of the way and tucked it into the laundry closet behind the kitchen.

Gabe entered through the front door this time, winked at

Alexis, then said, "Elsie, would you mind stepping out onto the porch for a moment? You have another visitor."

"Did that boy decide we needed *Santie* Claus at our table, too?" She shook her head but complied. "Let me grab a coat."

"We won't be long," Gabe said. He put his arm around Elsie's shoulder as if that would be warmth enough. It would have been for Alexis.

Arms wrapped around her middle, Alexis followed the two into the night.

At the end of the porch, at the top of the newly hewn ramp, sat Sebastian Brownell, wearing a new leather bomber jacket with a sheep's wool collar. Silver wings above the left breast pocket. A silver bar on each epaulette. Winged propellers on each lapel.

The eyes that had looked at life for more than ninety years turned to the woman who stepped closer to him. "Elsie! It's so good to see you."

Elsie hugged him a long moment.

The care center attendant behind the wheelchair suggested they get him inside. Elsie stepped out of the way. Alexis whispered to her, "Does he know you're his daughter? Or does he think you're the Elsie who took care of him during the war?"

"I don't know," she said. "It doesn't matter. He knows I love him."

Elsie followed the wheelchair into the house. Alexis stepped into Gabe's open arms. "How did you do this?"

"Impossible, huh?"

Sebastian's wheelchair was rolled into the house and into position at the now open head of the table. The vets watching pushed away from the table and stood to their feet, some more slowly than others. In unison, they saluted their fellow serviceman. Sebastian returned the salute. "As you were."

George caught it all on camera. He slipped in behind Gabe and Alexis and kept his camera rolling through the meal, stopping only briefly to munch on something passed to him. Elsie switched places and sat to her father's left for the meal, even though they said little to each other. The care unit worker sat to his right, helping when needed.

Henry proved a gracious conversationalist, drawing on his passion for history to make personal connections with the past lives of the veterans at his end of the table.

"As you were."

"What did you say?" Gabe slid a piece of cherry strudel onto one of twelve dessert plates waiting on the island.

"Sebastian's words. 'As you were.' Do you think any of us can go back to 'as we were'? I know I can't." She filled a second dish with strudel.

The pastry server in Gabe's hand stilled. He didn't look at Alexis but said, "I put in an offer on the house today."

"What house?"

"This house."

"You what?"

"I made Elsie an offer. I told her if she ever decided to sell, I wanted to be first in line and I'd pay full market value, whether that's next week . . . or twenty years from now."

Her middle tightened. "What did Elsie say?"

He resumed plating strudel. "She said she had her heart set on selling it to you."

Alexis leaned hard against the island, grateful for its locking wheels that kept it from plowing into the great room.

"I told her," Gabe said, "that's what I had in mind."

How necessary is breathing anyway?

"I'm going to take these first two to Elsie and Sebastian," Gabe said. "Sound good?"

"Sounds . . . very . . . good. Yes. Good. I'll be right behind you." She grabbed two more plates.

"*Beside* me sounds better."

THE CELLIST AND HARPIST left after the dessert had been served, on their way to the next of the three Christmas Eve services on their schedule for the night. The long-term care unit worker whispered to Alexis that Sebastian seemed to be tiring, despite the small smile that never left his face.

Henry stood and asked for a moment of attention. Alexis watched George change settings on his camera and train it on Mr. Ackerman.

"I have been honored to be included in this dinner.

Lieutenant Brownell, my family is indebted to you. You gave my grandparents a reason to go on hoping when their son, my father, was missing in action. They never stopped talking about you, or thanking God for you. This is from them."

He stood taller, drew a deep breath, and sang, his voice surprisingly strong and deep:

Stille Nacht! Heil'ge Nacht!
Alles schläft; einsam wacht
Nur das traute hoch heilige Paar.
Holder Knab' im lockigen Haar,
Schlafe in himmlischer Ruh!
Schlafe in himmlischer Ruh!

He drew another breath, closed his eyes, and continued:

Stille Nacht! Heilige Nacht!
Die der Welt Heil gebracht,
Aus des Himmels goldenen Höhn
Uns der Gnaden Fülle läßt sch´n
Jesum in Menschengestalt,
Jesum in Menschengestalt.

Amens circled the table.

"I don't believe I've ever heard the last verse you sang, Mr. Ackerman," Elsie said. "What did the words say?"

Sebastian Brownell took Elsie's hand in his. "You know this," he said.

Elsie's eyes apologized.

Sebastian's voice—cracked with age and emotion—said, "It's the verse that tells us, 'Mercy's abundance was made visible to us. Jesus in human form.' You sang it to me while I healed."

The other Elsie. Alexis dug in her pocket for a dry tissue for her friend.

Tears spilled. Elsie's weren't the only ones falling around the table.

"Yes. Yes, I did," Elsie said. "I remember now."

"My daughter only knew the English version," Sebastian said, his voice faint. "It, too, was a comfort." He turned his head toward the place where walls and ceiling meet. "I hope she found happiness."

Elsie laid her other hand on top of his. "She did. I assure you, she did."

Sebastian stared at her. From where she stood, Alexis could no longer see his expression. But the older man lifted his free hand and pointed to a spot high on her forehead. "Where did you get that scar? The war?"

"Yes, Papa. The war."

WITH ELSIE TUCKED into her own bed, the veterans enjoying the comfort of a guest room and family gatherings with various church members, and George headed home to ice his back, Alexis and Gabe finished the cleanup and settled in front of the fire.

"Exhausted?" Gabe asked.

"Every cell of my body."

"Put your feet on the coffee table. The home owner won't mind."

Alexis let the quiet overwhelm her with its peace. If she closed her eyes for a minute . . . No. Unfinished business remained. "You know I can't submit this video unless Elsie approves of that level of vulnerability broadcast to the world."

"I know. But I think her sons need to see it, at least."

"Me, too."

"And I think I'd like to watch it every Christmas from here on out."

"Me, too."

Gabe crossed his feet at the ankles on the rustic coffee table. "We should watch it together . . . since we've invested so much in the story."

"That's an idea." *Exhaustion apparently can make a person tremble all over.*

"I could, like, text you and ask how long it would take you to get from where you are to where I am every year," Gabe said. "You know. Christmas Eve. Five-thirty, maybe."

Alexis matched his crossed-feet position. "And I could, like, text you back and say, *It'll take me sixty seconds. Start the popcorn.*"

"Sounds like a plan."

"Mr. Langley, is that a proposal?"

He pulled his feet from the coffee table. "No! No. Goodness, no."

Heat crept up her neck. She'd thought—

"*This*"—he slid to the floor on one knee—"is a proposal."

EPILOGUE

Want to find out if Alexis got her show
on the Heart-and-Home Channel?

Visit RestoringChristmasNovel.com
and enter TELLMEMORE to find out!

ACKNOWLEDGMENTS

As so often happens, writing this story changed me. In some ways, I was the reclaimed island, the shutter hanging at an unnatural angle, the hardwood repurposed from the hayloft. Writing *Restoring Christmas* restored a sense of awe about what the holiday represents, and the people who represent the imaginary Alexis, Elsie, Gabe, and George in the story.

I'm grateful to the town of Algoma, Wisconsin, with all its charm, quirks, warmth, and history. It was easy to imagine the characters wanting to plant their roots along your sweet shore. I hope it won't be long before I'm again walking the Crescent Beach boardwalk. Thank you, Algoma Chamber of Commerce, for your enthusiasm about this story.

Thank you, Chip and Joanna Gaines (from HGTV's *Fixer Upper*). You don't know how much you influenced the characters, much less the concept of this novel. Or how your on-air dovetailed skills, perspectives, and relationship informed the creation of Gabe and Alexis and their love story. With each episode, you help remind me and your other viewers that two dramatically different personalities can—by God's grace—form one amazing couple.

My brother and sister-in-law who live in Algoma provided a home-away-from-home for research and details that helped enrich the setting. I can't be around them—or any of my other siblings and their families—without walking away inspired.

Thanks again, Dr. David Heegeman, for helping with medical details. Your exuberance over diseases and disorders would be disturbing if it didn't emanate from a heart for helping and professional excellence.

Sarah Sundin, I don't know who else would have been as quick to provide me with the historical possibilities I needed to make this story line work. It was a joy to tap in to your knowledge base and extract those gems. When readers get to the part in the story that brings unrelenting tears, please know you're part of the reason. (That made perfect sense, didn't it? And wasn't at all unnerving, right?)

Thank you, Worthy Publishing—the whole team—for allowing me the privilege of creating *Restoring Christmas*, and for your insights that strengthened it and strengthened me. Thanks for yet more stunning cover art and interior design. I will never forget hearing the kitten story as the Worthy team treated me to lunch. I almost left my chair to say, "Please, please, please say I can use that kitten fiasco in a book someday!" Here it is. Not quite as dramatic as the true story, but who would believe that one?

My agent, Wendy Lawton of Books & Such Literary Management, and my editor, Jamie Chavez, surround me with the best possible scaffolding for book creation and renovation.

Thank you for once again championing the stories I tell, and the author I am.

Becky Melby, you render me speechless with your ever-ready listening ear, your never-impatient critiquing, and your devotion to our friendship. That was kind of a little speech, but "speechless" was meant metaphorically.

Thank you, kids and grandkids, for your understanding and for being my best sales team.

I'm grateful for two beloveds—one has been my husband for more than four decades. His prayers for my writing melt my heart. The other is spelled with a capital *B*. My Beloved—Jesus. This book is about You. For You. And because of You, the Reclamation, Restoration, Renovation Expert whose birth is a story of its own.

Other Books by Cynthia Ruchti

(Non-Fiction)
Tattered and Mended: The Art of Healing the Wounded Soul
Ragged Hope: Surviving the Fallout of Other People's Choices

(Fiction)
A Fragile Hope
Song of Silence
An Endless Christmas
As Waters Gone By
All My Belongings
When the Morning Glory Blooms
They Almost Always Come Home

Contributing Author

(Devotionals and Journals)
Be Still and Let Your Nail Polish Dry: 365-Day Devotional Journal
Mornings with Jesus 2018
Mornings with Jesus 2017
Mornings with Jesus 2016
Mornings with Jesus 2015
Mornings with Jesus 2014
His Grace Is Sufficient . . . Decaf Is Not
A Joyful Heart
A Cup of Comfort for Writers

ABOUT THE AUTHOR

Cynthia Ruchti tells stories hemmed in hope. She's the award-winning author of more than eighteen books and a frequent speaker for women's ministry events. She serves as the professional relations liaison for American Christian Fiction Writers, helping retailers, libraries, and book clubs discover good books and connect with authors. She lives with her husband in Central Wisconsin.

I can't unravel, I'm

HEMMED in *hope*

Visit Cynthia at www.cynthiaruchti.com

IF YOU ENJOYED THIS BOOK, WILL YOU CONSIDER SHARING THE MESSAGE WITH OTHERS?

Mention the book in a blog post or through Facebook, Twitter, Pinterest, or upload a picture through Instagram.

Recommend this book to those in your small group, book club, workplace, and classes.

Head over to facebook.com/CynthiaRuchtiReaderPage, "LIKE" the page, and post a comment as to what you enjoyed the most.

Tweet "I recommend reading #RestoringChristmas by @cynthiaruchti // @worthypub"

Pick up a copy for someone you know who would be challenged and encouraged by this message.

Write a book review online.

Visit us at worthypublishing.com

 twitter.com/worthypub

 worthypub.tumblr.com

 facebook.com/worthypublishing

 pinterest.com/worthypub

 instagram.com/worthypub

 youtube.com/worthypublishing

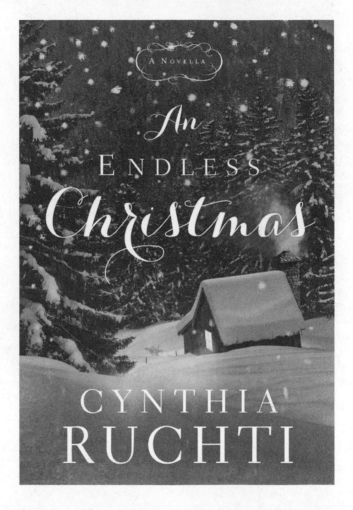